T0118453

# Dancers' Reunion

A Novel By

R. Douglas Johns

iUniverse, Inc.
Bloomington

# Dancers' Reunion


Book Cover Design by Evelyn Ventrchek/Crumbaker



This is a work of fiction. All of the characters, names, incidents, organizations, and dialogue in this novel are either the products of the author's imagination or are used fictitiously.

iUniverse books may be ordered through booksellers or by contacting:

iUniverse
1663 Liberty Drive
Bloomington, IN 47403
www.iuniverse.com
1-800-Authors (1-800-288-4677)



ISBN: 978-1-4620-3573-1 (sc)
ISBN: 978-1-4620-3574-8 (e)

Printed in the United States of America

iUniverse rev. date: 8/4/2011

## DEDICATION

This book is dedicated to dancers everywhere,
and to my wife Nancy, my muse.

## ACKNOWLEDGMENT

Bill Atalla, thank you for your
direction and motivation.

*"The best way to succeed is to discover what you love and find a way to offer it to others."*

OPRAH WINFREY

# Contents

RENO
THE BIGGEST LITTLE CITY IN THE WORLD

## Scene 1
# The Reunion

The night started out the same as every other Friday night; it just didn't end up that way. This night would bring three friends back together again and change their destinies forever.

It was early in the casino, not quite 8:00 PM, but the crowd seemed much larger and different in an unusual way. There were a whole lot more women than men. Not only were there more women, they all seemed exceptionally tall and, more than that, beautiful. Every one of them was worthy of a *Wow!*

The air in the room, which usually carried the acrid smell of cigars, was now filled with what seemed to be clouds of very different perfumes.

It was the kind of sensation that made your nose feel good and your mouth water.

The slot machines were ringing as loud as usual, but that was where usual ended. Mike, one of the regular customers at the main casino bar, was the first to voice it when he asked, "Did I die and go to heaven? Where did all these gorgeous angels come from all of a sudden?"

At first there were only a few women, and then dozens more appeared. Before long there were hundreds. Then, as fast as they came, they were gone.

In just moments, all of the women had filed into the showroom just across the casino. It wasn't until later everyone found out why they were there and why it had been such an enormous secret.

It was the most amazing display of beautiful females ever gathered under one roof. There they were, six hundred of the most beautiful, talented dancers and showgirls in the world. Literally, three decades of the best there were; the elite of the "Prima Donnas" were gathered together in one room.

They came from Paris, London, and as far away as Australia and South Africa. They came to attend the twenty-fifth anniversary of the opening of the greatest, largest, most extravagant show in the history of Reno.

It had a cast of hundreds and a budget in the millions. When the show opened in 1978 it was the talk of the town. No one had seen the likes of it since Flo Ziegfeld.

The cast members who showed up for the reunion that night were a spectacular group, and so very easy on the eye—"eye candy" to say the least.

Every single one of them was dressed to impress with their jewels, hats, long slinky designer outfits, and their incredible array of shoes.

A room full of shoes, "CFM" shoes, if you will. "CFM," as in "Come F—k me" shoes.

With that many beautiful women in one room, it's hard to believe that three of them would stand out so much, but they did. Three decades later, incredibly, they were still the best of the best. These three hadn't grown old, they had grown gorgeous.

They were ageless, all three of them. Twenty-five years ago, members of the original cast and crew voted on who they thought had the best legs, and Darcy won. The best tits category went to Sable, by a landslide, and the best body of all went to the unanimous choice, Amber. Then as now, it was the same three, even more so.

Darcy stood six feet tall and boasted 38-inch inseams. She still wore her mop of red hair in the Farrah Fawcett style, only longer. Her blouse was gold, toga-like, worn off one shoulder. She wore it over skin-tight leather pants, which only served to accentuate her black, Italian leather, thigh-high boots. The legs that brought her fame and fortune were every bit as good now as ever they had been.

Darcy's major difference was that as a young woman, she neither owned nor needed a bra. It wasn't because of women's lib or anything like that. When God engineered her, he used up all of her extra skin on those legs of hers and had nothing left for her chest.

However, with the magic of modern plastic

surgery, Darcy had improved her original design in a large way; very large, times two.

What didn't change at all were Darcy's eyes. They were the same almond, almost oriental shape as when she was young. Most stunning of all was their color. Describing them as emerald green wouldn't do her justice; her color of green didn't look natural.

Her eyes were such a brilliant green it looked like she was wearing tinted contacts. Add to the effect extremely long, full eyelashes and flowing red hair and what you came up with was sheer beauty, beauty that destined Darcy for a life in the very fast lane.

When Darcy saw Amber again at the reunion, it was a moment that seemed frozen in time. They were young back then; they were back to being just as young now. It was like time warped.

Twenty-five years just disappeared as soon as they turned around and saw each other. Amber and Darcy hugged, screamed, and then hugged some more. It wasn't until then that Amber noticed the differences and with a big smile asked Darcy, "Where did those come from?"

Darcy, smiling back replied, "I had to get the girls enlarged. You knew me when I was flat as a pancake. Cleavage was something I always wanted and I finally decided to do something about it once I was married. I'm not sure if I did it for my husband or for myself, but they have added a certain amount of spice to my life."

Amber, smiling, responded, "Well, it's about time, and you look absolutely beautiful."

Darcy added, "Thank you, but they came with extra responsibilities. I have to work out at the gym all the time just to keep the rest of me in shape".

Amber chimed in, "Isn't getting old a bitch? Can you remember the old days when the only exercise we needed was to dance two shows a night, six nights a week?"

With a twinkle in her eye, Darcy said, "It seems like only yesterday. Boy, time sure flew by."

Amber had a pizzazz that was all her own, an incredible lust for life. She lit up every place she went and everyone she touched. It is an extremely old cliché, but no one else deserved it as much, "To know her was to love her."

Amber's face didn't come equipped with frown muscles. Dimples and smiles were her blessings. She seemed to have an aura of goodness around her. Amber never did drugs, but if you knew her, you might find that hard to believe, she was so full of energy.

Amber's body was like an hourglass, even now. Back then she had the unbelievable measurements of 36-19-36. Not quite the same now, but still outstanding.

If Barbie had been a real person, her name would have been Amber. Amber was also endowed with what an African American reporter friend described as the best ass he had ever seen on a white woman.

Like Darcy, Amber had incredible eyes. Amber's were gold at times and light green at times. It was difficult to tell if her clothes or her mood changed her eyes' colors, but they really did seem to change.

Her eyes were huge and gave Amber what most

people called the best "stage presence" of the entire cast. When she was out there, she seemed to fill up the stage all by herself.

If eyes are the mirror of the soul, hers were the eyes of a very old mirror. Amber truly was an "old soul."

Even though her eyes had a tendency to sparkle, like those of an Irishman spinning a tale, they were amazingly soft, like a mother's smile. Amber also had so many dimples they should have been called, "trimples."

Suddenly, almost like it was rehearsed, Sable showed up, and it was just like old times. Three best friends together again, as if twenty five years had not passed. Sable took one look at Darcy and blurted, "You've got tits."

Darcy said with a chuckle, "I always wanted tits like you and Amber. Now, what do you think?", as she turned sideways with her hands on her hips and shot Sable a profile view.

Amber responded, "That's funny, I always wanted to have long legs like you."

Sable echoed, "Me, too. If I had those legs and these tits, I would have conquered the world." The three of them broke out laughing. They had a lot of catching up to do, and they looked forward to hearing each other's adventures over the years.

Sable looked much the same but had aged more than the other two. Sable's skin was still the whitest of whites; her hair was the blackest of blacks. The combination set off her huge, ice-blue eyes. If you can recall Disney's cartoon character, Snow White, Sable was her personification. She, too, was built like the proverbial "brick house."

The three of them had tried to stay in touch over the years, but the stress and demanding lives they all led had reduced a lifelong friendship to Christmas cards and little more, until now. The love was still there, but their destinies had been so completely different. From now on, that would change.

## Scene 2
# The Bleu Belles

Amber, Darcy and Sable were "Bleu Belles." They were three of many promising young stars in a large ensemble of dancers and show girls represented by Madame Bleu Belle, the true "queen of dance." Just to be a Bleu Belle was to be recognized as one of the most talented dancers, showgirls, and performers anywhere.

Madame Bleu began her long and illustrious career as a dancer in the Ziegfeld Follies. In her prime she took her place at center stage as a lead dancer and thrilled audiences as well as Flo Ziegfeld himself.

An irreparable knee injury that came as a result of a failed lift ended her dancing career too soon. The injury never healed properly and she walked with some difficulty and the aid of a cane the remainder of her years.

Even so, Madame Bleu's love for the stage and her fellow performers evolved into the creation of her empire, an empire that would cover the earth in her lifetime.

When show producers anywhere in the world needed a cast of tall, gorgeous dancers and/or showgirls, it was Madame Bleu they turned to.

By the way, if you didn't know it, there was a difference—a huge difference—between dancers and showgirls. If you called a dancer a showgirl, you were certain to regret it. Dancers took pride in their ability to perform and were the center of the visual experience.

The showgirls were the frame. However, to Madame Bleu, they were all the same; they were her children.

Paris was her home when she wasn't on the road. Her residence was an old converted mansion that allegedly belonged to one of Napoleon's favorite chefs. It was elaborate, to say the least.

Madame Bleu's home was her passion, second only to dance. She spent a fortune remodeling and restoring it, including antiques she bought all over the world. She named it, "C'est Magnifique."

Madame Bleu never married. Her home was her man and more than man enough for her. She had enough "boy toys" over the years to amuse her. Madame Bleu neither had the time nor the will to share her world with one man. That would have complicated a life that was already extremely complex.

Speaking of complex, at the peak of her career, her empire included over a thousand performers actively working, with half as many more in transition. They were appearing all over the world. She had performers in Paris, Berlin, London, New York, Las Vegas, Reno and as far away as South Africa.

Madame Bleu received a piece of every one of their paychecks. Not a big piece, she wasn't greedy, but a piece just the same. Over a thousand pieces every month added up to a considerable amount. Besides, some of her performers, if not most, had been with her all of their careers.

Loyalty was Madame Bleu's favorite asset. She considered it a necessary two-way street. She gave it and she demanded it in return. God help the performer who did her wrong. There wasn't a professional dancer anywhere in the world who didn't know her or know of her.

The producers, as well, knew the potential of her wrath; it was legendary. Woe is unto he who decided to hire a performer who was on Madame Bleu's "black list." That producer's chances of surviving in that business were extremely limited.

She wasn't exactly a monopoly, but close, very close. She was Madame Bleu. She was also one of the wealthiest women in all of France, and the most powerful force in the dance world for nearly forty years.

She was what brought Darcy, Amber, and Sable together then, and now they were together one more time. All three of their lives had been looked over by guardian angels, and now, together, their destinies were about to mesh again.

# Scene 3
# The Auditions

Of them all, Amber became Madame Bleu's favorite. Like Madame Bleu, everyone who knew Amber knew she had something special that exploded when she hit the stage. More than anyone else, Amber reminded Madame Bleu of herself in her prime. She had the same love for the magic that comes from inside.

Amber first learned of the auditions for Madame Bleu through the dancer's grapevine. The audition was held in Los Angeles and drew hundreds of hopeful dancers.

Word of it spread like wildfire through all of the dance studios on the west coast. Rumor had it that they were going to select over a hundred dancers for a big show, but no one knew where it was going to be.

When Amber showed up to the audition that day in May, she happened to be standing between two gorgeous, statuesque Amazons, both of whom were well over the minimum required height of five feet eight.

Madame Bleu slowly walked over to Amber with her cane in hand and stated, “You’re not five eight. I’m five eight, and you simply are not.”

Amber, barely five feet six, stretched as tall as she could and nervously replied, “I do know how tall I am, but I really want to audition. I’ve worked all my life for this chance”. Then Amber smiled impishly with an expression that touched Madame Bleu’s heart.

Despite Amber’s height, Madame Bleu seemed to notice something special about her. That keen old eye told her to give Amber a chance, for some reason unknown to anyone else. She turned to Amber and said, “Okay, show me what you’ve got.”

The rest, as they say, is history.

This was what Amber dreamed about and prepared for all of her life. The thousands of hours she spent working her butt off in dance classes and practicing prepared her for this moment. Her time was now. This was it.

She knew every count, every move, and every single step. If dreams did come true, hers was a blink of an eye away.

Amber felt something throb in her chest when they cued her music. In an instant she could feel the music deep inside. The beat and the rhythm were telling her to fly.

Amber started with her back to the room, pulsating to the beat; she spun around and took over the stage. She leapt so high she seemed to be defying gravity itself. Her center was so strong that her pirouettes were unstoppable.

The other dancers nervously waiting to audition could not believe their eyes when Amber did her signature move, spinning while holding her right leg up against her body, pointing it straight to heaven, turning again and again.

From that pirouette she flew through the air like a gazelle and then moved across the floor in a rhythmic explosion, showing her incredible flexibility and agility.

Amber moved perfectly with the music, she became the music with grace, elegance, and strength. Her ability to grab the audience's attention was something to behold.

Amber's performance was so overwhelming that at its end, the entire room went totally silent. Not one single sound from anywhere or anyone. It was an enormous silence that lasted only for a few moments, extended moments.

The silence was broken when Madame Bleu rose to her feet, clapping, with the warmest expression of admiration glowing on her face.

It was then, and only then, that everyone in the room went wild. The other dancers, choreographers, crew, and even the janitors were on their feet screaming and clapping. Every single person in the room was a part of it.

Because Madame Bleu led the way in the standing ovation, Amber noticed no one else. In her moment of glory, all Amber could do was smile at that old icon who was just as caught up in the magic of the moment, smiling back. They both had tears in their eyes.

All of the rest of them stood and applauded so long and so loud, the stage manager eventually had to rudely take over to get back to auditions. Amber and Madame Bleu stood for a moment longer and it was obvious they adored each other.

Amber did a dancer's bow from the waist out of respect as much as thanks for the opportunity.

Amber had her moment, and she more than nailed it. She walked away with that feeling of accomplishment that only comes when you reach into your soul and grasp every bit of knowledge, experience, effort, and the dreams you have to offer, and then the rest goes the way you always pictured it.

She was completely spent, but even so, she walked away on cloud nine.

# Scene 4
# Fast Friends

As Amber left the stage, she met Darcy for the first time. Darcy came over just to tell her, "Wow! What you just did was nothing short of amazing. I couldn't take my eyes off you, and it's obvious no one else could either."

Amber, still out of breath, smiled her hugest smile and said, "I hope it was good enough to get a job in a show somewhere. More than anything I want to work for Madame Bleu."

Darcy beamed right back at her proudly announcing, "I'm so excited, I just signed a contract to work for Madame Bleu in a huge new production show in Reno. Now I've got to move in a hurry. We open rehearsals there in two weeks and I'm just not ready."

Darcy actually stood a full head taller than Amber, but at that moment they seemed to be looking each other straight in the eye.

As they were talking, the company manager walked up and took Amber to the side. What he offered her was the standard contract for dancers. At the same time, he told her rehearsals began in two weeks in Reno, if she was available.

To say she was blown away would be a gross understatement. Amber, almost in disbelief, said, "Am I available? You bet. I am so available."

This meant she could quit the other profession dancers usually have; no more waiting tables for her.

Darcy was watching. When Amber started jumping up and down, Darcy knew Amber got the job.

Amber practically floated over to Darcy, grinning from ear to ear and stated, "I'm going to be working in Reno with you. I can't wait. This is my first real professional chance to dance. I just can't believe I'm actually going to get paid to dance. I'd do it for free, hell, I'd pay them. Do I seem a little out of control?"

Darcy screamed with delight and said, "Let's go out and celebrate." Quite possibly, somehow, Darcy had found a girlfriend. It was Amber's day, but for the first time in Darcy's life, she had a friend that was female.

As soon as the paperwork was signed, the two new buds took off to celebrate. And celebrate they did. Neither one of them was a big drinker, but on that night they did what you do in Los Angeles when you celebrate: they went to dinner and hit the night clubs.

This was a chance for Darcy and Amber to get to know each other.

Darcy matured early and she never had the kind of girlfriend most young women enjoy, until Amber. Darcy humbly explained, "My appearance has always made other women feel extremely threatened, even jealous. When I was around, women kept their men on a short leash."

"I didn't want it that way, but I've never had a close girlfriend. I was six feet tall in the eighth grade.

I was taller than almost everyone, including the teachers."

Darcy continued, "Men, on the other hand, loved my long legs. I was a jock and an avid fan of every team in Los Angeles. I was a semiprofessional volleyball player and I love to surf."

"Between my red hair, green eyes, long legs, and a year-round tan, I got all the male attention I could handle. That part of my life was as good as it gets. Men had never been a problem for me—only women, until now. I'm so happy we met."

Amber had never been intimidated by other women, for a lot of good reasons. That is not to say Amber was intimidating. She was quite the opposite. She was engaging, encouraging, and, when it came to friendship, she was as "easy as Sunday morning."

To Darcy, Amber was the answer to a lifelong prayer.

That night they danced in the disco until everyone went home and there was no more music. Amber and Darcy laughed and talked and told stories for hours on end.

## Scene 5
# The Apartment

Two weeks later they were roommates moving into their new apartment in Reno, Nevada, the "Biggest Little City in the World."

For the first time in her life, Darcy was living on her own, not at her parents' home. She never had a waterbed, but they were the rage at the time, so she got one. It even came with a brass headboard. Being a fan of Dylan, it seemed to mean something to her, as in, "Lay across my big brass bed."

The apartment itself was an upstairs flat that shared a common landing with the apartment next door. It was just off campus from the university and was extremely affordable. On the day they were moving in, their neighbors were also moving in.

One of them, Ramon, was tall, dark, and extremely handsome. Then they met his roommate/lover, who happened to be a gay dwarf named Izzy.

Amber was the first to introduce herself. "Hi, I'm Amber. Looks like we're your new neighbors. This is my roommate, Darcy. We're so excited. We're starting rehearsals this week for a big new production show here in town."

Ramon responded, "I'm one of the dancers in the show, too, and I'm scared to death about rehearsals."

When Darcy asked why, Ramon responded, "Haven't you ever heard of the producer/director? He has a reputation of being an absolute monster." The two girls looked at each other and the three of them broke out in a nervous laughter.

Out of curiosity, Darcy asked Izzy, "Are you in the show, too?"

Izzy laughed out loud and said, "No, girlfriend, but I am the greatest hair stylist in Reno."

Amber responded with delight, "It's my lucky day. Will you cut my hair?"

Izzy, with his sparkling eyes and his special childish grin, said, "I would love to, girlfriend, any time you're ready, I'm available.

Then he turned to Darcy and asked, "How about you honey?"

Darcy thought for minute and replied, "No, I'm good for now."

As time went by, the four of them became the best of friends and rarely locked their doors. Somebody was always running in and out to borrow or share just about anything. It was more like four girlfriends than four girlfriends ever were.

During the first three weeks of rehearsal, Amber went from a shoulder-length brunette to a short and sassy blonde at the hands of Izzy. Amber got braver and Izzy got more creative and more hair hit the floor.

During one of the hair creations, after having a couple of glasses of wine, Izzy admitted, "My real name is Isaiah. My father named me. He was a preacher. I guess I didn't turn out quite the way he hoped." With that he broke into his very own delightful chuckle.

Izzy was a character, to say the least. He knew everyone who mattered in Reno, and everyone who mattered knew him.

Even though Izzy might have been small on the outside, he had some enormous features. He had a heart as big as King Kong, and he had these great big, weepy, blue eyes that could grab your heart.

When Izzy was happy, and he was almost always happy, those eyes of his turned up and on, and he became more like a leprechaun than a dwarf.

Izzy was one of those people who brought more to life than he took from it. If one word could describe him, "giver" would be that word. Izzy gave of himself like few others ever did. Everyone absolutely adored him.

The second weekend in their new apartment, Darcy's parents came to visit. Her father was a real estate broker and extremely domineering in an overpowering way. He was a handsome man, but very dark and distant. He was a hulking presence in this room, much like any other room he was ever in.

Her mother, on the other hand, was a quiet woman, beautiful beyond her years. She had a way of looking down at her hands when she spoke, and she spoke so rarely and so softly that most people hardly noticed. It was a characteristic of hers; she always seemed lost in her thoughts, withdrawn.

Mr. and Mrs. Roberts were very wealthy, as in very, very wealthy. Her father was more than a little full of himself and it showed.

Darcy and her mother could pass for sisters. Her father, on the other hand, bore Darcy no resemblance whatsoever. It was a burden her mother explained to Darcy years later, at the end of her mother's life.

For now, they were sitting in the living room of Darcy's new dream apartment having tea, when the front door burst open. It was Izzy, the gay dwarf, and he was running around clad only in a G-string, screaming at the top of his lungs that Ramon was going to kill him.

Just then, Ramon came running in, also wearing a G-string and nothing else. He was waving a butcher knife around.

Ramon proceeded to chase Izzy around the kitchen island, both of them screaming at each other. They made two complete revolutions, then back out to their place, slamming the door behind them as they left. It had a kind of tornado effect.

Darcy, caught off guard, kind of laughed, choked, and ejected a mouthful of tea. Her mom looked at her and gasped, "What in the world was that?"

Embarrassed, Darcy tried to explain, saying, "Oh, those are just our new neighbors. They are a bit unusual, aren't they?"

Her father jumped to his feet and immediately did his best to assume charge. He barked at Darcy, saying, "You are out of here. This will never do. I insist you move to a more suitable place, no matter where, even if I have to pay for it, no matter what it costs."

He absolutely demanded that Darcy prepare to move immediately. He started snapping out orders and became more than offensive, telling Darcy that this was his decision. Raising his voice, he boomed it was, "Not negotiable," as he had at so many critical times in her past.

Finally, Darcy stood up to him for the first time in her life. She was terribly frightened, shaking like a leaf. Neither she nor her mom had ever dared to confront him before, but this was different.

Darcy couldn't stop herself. The words just jumped out of her mouth. She said, "I love you Dad, but the time for you to run my life is over." On a roll, her voice grew louder when she said, "It's over right here and right now."

In a softer voice she told him, "Dad, I'm a professional dancer now, and I'm going to live like a dancer. More than anything in my life, I want to be a part of something that I've earned and deserve, not something that was given to me on a silver platter, like the rest of my life has been."

Darcy built up a head of steam and when her father saw the look in her eyes, he knew Darcy wasn't going to be his little girl ever again.

To him, it was an enormous loss. His Darcy was

one of two females he had ever loved; no matter how poorly he expressed it. His wife had always been so distant, even aloof to him. He knew his wife had always been true to him since their marriage, but he never felt like she loved him, not at all like he worshipped her.

The love of the two women in his life had now led to the worst kind of disappointment. He felt like a failure, and in retrospect, he should. Real love involved understanding and accepting, things he had never been good at.

To Darcy, it was the biggest, most important step in her life, a life that had always been more or less that of a puppet, with him pulling the strings.

When she was finished, she felt exhausted, but even more so, she felt like the heaviest weight was suddenly removed from her shoulders.

There was an eerie quiet in the room that was interrupted only when her mother gave out a huge sigh, ran over to Darcy, and gave her the biggest of tear-filled hugs.

In almost the same move, with tears in her eyes, her mother turned on the man she had been married to all of her life. She announced, "Darcy is right and you better back off." She added, "This is not negotiable!" as loud as she dared, which was ten times louder than Darcy or her father had ever heard before.

With that, it was done. In a single moment, two women were emancipated and things were never to be the same for either of them.

## Scene 6
# Roommates' Secrets

On the first day of rehearsals, chaos ruled. The casino as well as the showroom were still under construction when in poured nearly four hundred performers. Most of them were complete strangers.

There were singers, dancers, showgirls, specialty acts, costume designers, choreographers, and stagehands, all waiting nervously to see what would happen next.

Suddenly, this enormous voice came booming out of the loudspeakers. The voice was the one they all would become too familiar with in the weeks to come. This time his voice mesmerized them all when he said, "Ladies and gentlemen, welcome to the greatest show on Earth!"

In the confusion that followed, they were all herded into their individual departments. Dancers were in one group, singers in another, etc. Once they separated, the work began immediately.

Sable and Amber were dancers in the same line. They were called "ponies" because they were shorter than the other dancers. However, the ponies carried most of the real dancing in the show. They weren't really paid as leads, but when it came to selling the dance numbers, there they were, stage center.

Sable and Amber were both such incredible dancers that they were in every major number, right out front. It was only natural that they became competitors, a role they both hated, but learned to relish. Instead of the *Showgirls* movie version, where dancers tried to destroy each other, these two were there to help the other shine.

Even in rehearsals, it was obvious those two were a different breed. Amber was such a quick study, choreographers adored her. Sixteen counts and she was ready.

After two days of rehearsals Amber knew not only

her part, but everyone's part in her group. Sable was the same. There just wasn't anyone like them. Dance was the love of their young lives.

Even though they were complete opposites, they were so much alike. Born and raised in London, Sable was so British. Amber, on the other hand, grew up in Detroit and was so Motown.

Although they were raised half a world apart, they were cut from the same cloth, they were dancers. It's what they did, dance defined them. It was what they were, what they wanted to be.

Their relationship morphed into a partnership with amazing results. Most of the show's dances were done in groups of six or more at a time. These two were the exception.

In almost every number they were in, the two of them were featured at stage center. They were both amazingly beautiful and had incredible bodies, and no one could dance like them. No one could come close.

During rehearsals Sable had fallen in lust with one of the male lead dancers, James. After one night together, they realized she was good for him, but for some reason, not quite good enough. Even though it wouldn't end well, and it didn't, they tried. Three weeks later, she was out and another dancer named Patrick was in.

The next day, Amber, for the first time, saw Sable looking like she had been in a train wreck.

Worried, Amber took Sable aside. When Amber asked what was wrong, Sable broke down crying. Through her tears she blurted out, "I don't have a man and I don't even have a place to live."

The next words out of Amber's mouth were, "C'mon, we've got room," and c'mon Sable did.

That's how it came to be. Three of the most incredible women in the world were roommates. Not only were they roommates, they were best friends, confidantes and sisters, through thick and thin.

They became so close, they could discuss anything together.

One night, while the three of them were sitting around watching TV and drinking wine, Sable suddenly popped out with, "Have either one of you ever had a real orgasm?"

Darcy, after almost spilling her wine asked, "Why are you asking?"

Sable reddened when she admitted, "I never have, and I think there's something seriously wrong with me."

Amber in utter surprise asked, "Never?"

Sable told them, "I had sex for the first time when I was fourteen, my step-father raped me and it was a horrifying experience that scarred me for life. Since then I've had, let's say, more than a few partners. Nothing works for me, I'm afraid nothing ever will. Please tell me I'm not the only one."

Darcy, smiling, told Sable, "Sorry, Sable, that's never been a problem for me. You can count the number of lovers I've had on both hands, but in all honesty, all but a couple of them were extremely successful in that department."

Amber, in an effort to lessen Sable's concern, told her, "I was so busy with dancing that I didn't lose my virginity until I was almost twenty, so I don't have all that much to talk about."

Amber continued, "I was involved with a guitar player for a while and the sex was phenomenal. Dave was the first man I ever made love with. When I met him I thought I was in love. But the other two weren't so great. So what I'm trying to say Sable, it's not your fault. When you meet the right person, it will happen and then you will find out what all the shouting is about."

Sable ended that part of the conversation with, "This is extremely embarrassing, and I hope it will always be our secret."

Amber thought for a moment and confided, "I guess I have my own secret. The guitar player I just told you about was so patient. We dated for six months but as much as he wanted to, I was just too scared to go all the way. All my friends had been doing it for years but not me."

Amber was embarrassed but went on, "I was such a mess; I didn't know what to do. Finally my mom asked me what was wrong with me and I broke down crying and told her everything."

Amber remembered her mom's reaction, "She sat and looked at me for a while and she smiled with tears running down her cheeks and said she had no idea I was still a virgin. Then she asked me, "Girl, what are you waiting for?"

"She even came up with a plan. It was her idea to drive me to Dave's house and drop me off and tell my dad I was at a slumber party with my girlfriends. That way he would not wonder where I was all night. Looking back, that was a secret I never shared with anyone but my mom."

With a sweet smile Amber added, "It wasn't easy on my mom. She told me later when she was driving away she looked in her rear view mirror to see me, but what she didn't expect to see was her make-up running down her face."

Darcy went even further, "Well, I can top that secret. Something happened to me once that I am so ashamed of. I was barely sixteen and taking jazz classes and it really amazed me when my instructor, the greatest dancer I had ever seen asked me to stay after class."

Darcy paused for a few moments and then went

on, "I don't know if I should tell you anymore, it's just too humiliating."

Sable shot in, "Come on, that's not fair. I told you something personal about me."

Amber said, "Yea, come on Darcy."

Darcy was not able to look them in the eyes when she continued, "All of the other dancers had already left and it was just he and I."

"I was scared to death. There were so many fantastic dancers in my class; I thought he was going to tell me he hated my dancing."

"Instead he said I had talent but I needed a private tutor. He said he would take me under his wing but only if I would do everything he told me to do. I was so flattered, I was giddy."

Looking directly at Sable and Amber, biting her lip Darcy said, "When I told him I would do anything, he told me to prove it."

"When I asked how, he told me to strip and make love to him right there."

Again Darcy hesitated. Sable who was now sitting on the edge of her seat said, "Don't stop now, what's wrong with that? Do you think you're the first dancer that ever got it on with her instructor?"

Darcy, in an even softer voice said, "It was great up to a point, we made love and we danced and it was weeks of amazing fun. I was so infatuated with him."

"It was then that he told me he was tutoring another student and that he wanted to see us perform together. I naively thought he meant dancing."

Looking down Darcy added, "How dumb could I be? The next night in the studio the three of us were there together and he was showing Christine and I some new choreography when he pulled out some pills. He said they would give us energy."

"Within minutes it felt like I was in a dream. The three of us were dancing in front of the mirrors and flowing with the music."

Darcy continued, "Then they started taking their clothes off. At first I didn't know what to do, there they were, both naked. Then he told me to take off my clothes too."

"I was so young and so self-conscience about my lack of breasts, I was embarrassed but I did what he said and took my clothes off too."

"Then he ordered Christine and me to have sex with each other. That was my first and only time with a woman, but it obviously wasn't hers".

"After watching for a while, he joined in. It seemed like it went on for hours. Remembering what I did that night still haunts me. I was only sixteen."

"It wasn't until a couple of years later I found out the two of them did the same thing to a bunch of other young girls. They really were sexual predators."

Amber reacted with, "Wow, sex at sixteen was the farthest thing from my mind."

Sable chuckled and said, "Big deal, so you had a ménage a trois. If that's your most embarassing moment, I would love to trade you my most embarassing moment and no, I'm not going to tell you about that one, not now anyway."

## Scene 7

# Five, Six, Seven, Eight — Rehearsals

Rehearsals lasted three months and were grueling, fatiguing, long, difficult, and almost impossible. They did, however, make for some of the most memorable moments.

From day one, it just didn't seem possible that it would ever get done, let alone in time for the show to open when planned. Carpenters, electricians, plumbers, and God knows who else were everywhere.

Elevators were installed three stories above and four stories below the stage. Guys ran around with their tool belts and measuring tapes, and still rehearsal went on.

Once completed, those elevators were designed to lift complete sets from storage below in a matter of minutes. One set included a full-size DC-10 airplane that had eight performers standing on each wing as it moved toward the audience with landing lights on. That was just the opening number.

Justin, one of the stagehands, told one of the other crew members that he was amazed at the change in the entire appearance of the cast, once the show actually went on.

At first, he was disappointed because he had fantasized about meeting and working with all those gorgeous, young beauties. Justin envisioned coffee together and imagined hanging out with them during lunches in the cafeteria.

He was a young, single, horny stagehand. Some of that might seem redundant. What left him wanting was the way the female dancers looked during rehearsals.

There was little or no make-up and the standard attire was dancers' sweats, because that was what the dancers did during rehearsals: sweat. When you spend most of your waking hours banging across a hardwood floor the size of a football field, at full speed, vanity has absolutely no place at all.

As it turned out, with the exception of the dressers, Justin, like most of the stage and construction crew, had very little to do with the dancers. They ended up at opposite ends of the spectrum.

However, at the first full dress rehearsal, Justin was completely blown away by the amazing transformations he witnessed in the dancers firsthand.

For the first time, Justin saw every single one of those young, gorgeous females in full-blown stage make-up, "Bambi" eyelashes and all. That's not to mention the costumes, or lack thereof, and the beautiful bodies that were on full display.

Justin hardly recognized most of them, standing there with his mouth open. As they walked by him, they smiled at him and each one seemed to be enjoying his awe in a very special way.

Moments like that are rare in most people's lives.

He had his that night, and a lot of them shared it with him.

Finally, one of the older veteran stagehands walked up behind him and said, "Justin, you're embarrassing the rest of the crew, please close your mouth."

The seating in the room was arranged coliseum style and could accommodate over two thousand people. In short, it was a big room for its time.

Considering that some of the girl dancers from Europe were as young as sixteen, the experience was bigger than life itself. Most of the cast were so very young, as well as inexperienced. It was an exciting time, a time that led to memories most of them would cherish forever.

The producer and brains behind the show was Bob Gordon. He ruled over his room like a tyrant. In some ways, he was more like a blacksmith. The more he pounded on his metal, the harder it got. He pounded and pounded and then pounded some more.

It was flesh and bones, not metal, that he pounded and pushed beyond physical limits. The closer they got to opening night, the tougher it got. What were blisters got worse. Injuries came and didn't leave. Spasms and cramps became a way of life.

He was both a genius and an arrogant ass.

The genius reputation came with successfully producing the biggest and best stage shows of modern times. Everything Bob Gordon touched turned to gold. He had the money, imagination, experience, and the balls to do things nobody else had done since Ziegfeld. He had become a millionaire many times over as a result. There was a lot of money in dance—just not for the dancers.

The arrogant ass part came from his rudeness.

During rehearsals, he treated the performers like they were dirt. The slightest mistake would bring down his wrath. To make it worse, he had a microphone. What came out of that microphone was acid, ridicule, and pure agony and sent more than a few performers to their knees in tears.

The things he said were anything but humorous.

Bob Gordon's stage was his whole world, and he wanted perfection and, more importantly, he wanted it now.

Bob Gordon, "God," as the dancers called him, put all of the construction workers in their place the first day they were all in the same room. Over the loud speakers, he boomed, "Will all of you working ants stay out of the way of these true artists, *please*?"

Darcy was there. She would never forget the time she completely blew her part, only to hear his booming voice over the loudspeakers say, "Darcy, go flush yourself down the toilet."

That moment was the most humiliating of her entire life. It happened during the first days of rehearsal and proud as she was of everything else in her life, at that moment she was crushed.

For the rest of her life, Sable remembered his exact words to her after her first big error. She totally missed her spot and ended up bumping into another dancer who just happened to be in the right place.

God boomed across the room, "Sable, if you were

half as good a dancer as you think you are, you would be twice as good a dancer as you really are."

She was so insulted and hurt, she wanted to quit right there. It also infuriated her so much she set her jaw, determined to prove what a jerk he was. Mission accomplished. She never got singled out again.

Amber did, however. When it was her turn to hear the "wrath of God," she had missed her mark because she was watching out for her younger dancer friends. Some of the younger girls were having extreme difficulty learning their parts.

Because Amber was such a quick study, she knew each part, so she stayed after rehearsal and coached them in the parts they couldn't get. Extra hours, but it was worth it. Worth it, until she got so involved watching out for the younger girls doing their parts, she more or less blew her own.

The next voice she heard sounded like God in the movie *The Ten Commandments* saying, "When did we start hiring midgets who can't dance?" She almost died.

Their neighbor and friend Ramon, who wasn't all that manly, was so embarrassed when that same nasty voice yelled over the loudspeakers, "Ramon, you dance like a dime-store queen." Ramon seemed to shrink in size.

In summary, if Bob Gordon could have sent flames through his microphone, he would have. Without that, he did the next best thing: he fired off words that left brands on the memories of his cast, brands that would last a lifetime. Long after he was gone, those brands would still be there.

Out of the chaos, an amazing show evolved, but not without some bizarre mishaps along the way.

Once was when the lion, mascot of the hotel, was ceremoniously lifted in his gold-plated cage from the stage to an elevation about thirty feet above the orchestra pit. To the delight of everyone, as if on cue, he let out a deafening roar.

However, he then proceeded to lift his rear leg and sprayed urine over a large area, which was anything but a delight to anyone within range.

On another occasion, an equipment malfunction

almost resulted in serious injuries to dozens of performers, including Amber and Sable. They were all posed on a platform on an elevator below the main floor.

What went wrong was when the platform they were on began to rise, the floor above them failed to open and they were nearly crushed. Amber was the first to realize what the danger was and screamed for help.

Her scream alerted a fast-thinking technician who realized what was happening in time to hit the override button. That stopped the elevator just moments before what would have been a disaster.

On still another occasion, one of the dancers in a top hat and cane number stepped on a trap door that wasn't latched properly, and he just sort of disappeared. One of the other dancers in the number, Ramon, without missing a beat, reached down and pulled him out and the show went on. It was as if it was planned that way.

It even impressed god, who rarely said anything encouraging, when he purred over the speaker, "Nice work Ramon" at the end of the number.

Ramon bought all the drinks that night; he was so proud.

The same trap door opened by mistake on still another number. This time one of the horses pulling a Roman chariot fell through. After his harness was disconnected, the parade went on. When the number ended, the stagehands were able to get the horse out safely without any injuries.

In another instance, there was some nastiness that went on between the male dancers, some of whom were gay and some straight. They really did not care for each other. Since there were far more of the gay dancers, the huge advantage went their way. They were constantly setting traps for their counterparts.

As a result, by the time the dress rehearsals came around, there were very few of the straight dancers left.

During the first full dress rehearsal, everyone was moving around at hyper speed. The straight dancer who was their prime target got his. He was extremely unpopular among the gay dancers because he made a point of gay-bashing them whenever he could.

After the opening number, he had a fast change into a different colored costume, which meant he had to change G-strings to match. What he didn't know was that moments before, one of the gay dancers had put glue into the new G-string he changed into.

He didn't realize it until it was too late, much too late. By the time that number was over and he got back to the dressing room, his pubic area felt like it was on fire.

His G-string had to be removed in the emergency room at a local hospital. He suffered some chemical burns, and that was it. He quit and never danced professionally again.

The show evolved that way. No one person was better than the others, or there were consequences, and there were always consequences.

On the other hand, some of the consequences were the complete opposite for the female dancers, singers, and showgirls. Most of the females were great friends.

It was at a time when the ladies were spoiled by the local community in an enormous way. The female dancers and showgirls were treated like show business royalty everywhere they went. Before their arrival, Reno had never seen anything like what they had to offer.

Dancers cut tapes at local bank openings and their pictures and articles were in the local newspaper almost every day. Darcy loved seeing her face on the front page of the local paper, she had a real taste of "star power," and somehow she knew it was only the beginning.

Most of the dancers had never been treated like royalty before, but they learned to handle it well.

Beautiful, young women from all over the world came to the, "Biggest Little City in the World," and they did it with style.

## Scene 8

# Naked at the Pool

The apartment complex they lived in was so inexpensive and convenient that most of the dancers lived there. When they first moved in it was summer, and summer in Reno is great for suntans.

That created a problem; no tan lines were permitted on the dancers who performed topless. Show up with tan lines and face a steep fine. A second violation could lead to dismissal.

Since the dancers made up almost half of the apartments rented at the time, Amber and Darcy came up with the idea and they asked the managers if one of the two pools could be restricted to the dancers and no one else.

The pool they really wanted was surrounded by a six foot, ivy covered fence and would provide some privacy.

Management agreed, and the next few days that pool became the place where you might stumble upon eighty or ninety beautiful young bodies attired only in the obligatory G-strings.

Unfortunately, they were stumbled upon by a couple of hormonally unbalanced teenage boys.

One of the boys' mothers overheard them talking on the phone to their other buddies, trying to get them to come over for a two-dollar peek.

When she decided to investigate on her own, she was amazed at what she saw—so much so, she called the police.

When the police dispatcher put out the call, "Public disturbance—dozens of naked, young women reported," every unit in the area, including patrol cars, motorcycles, and even horse-mounted officers from the nearby university responded.

When they got there, they called for back-up,

advising that there were far too many “perps” to transport without additional help.

Literally half of Reno’s finest responded. So did the news media. Flash bulbs were popping and film was rolling. It was a circus that went on for hours. No one was allowed to leave.

Sable & Amber happened to be at the pool that day. Amber had a towel but Sable didn’t. When one of the officers took off his shirt to help Sable out, he was booed by on-lookers, but he was rewarded by the look in Sables eyes. She did have a thing for men in uniform.

It wasn’t until later in the day that the local district attorney decided to release them all with a warning.

THE Magic Factor

## Scene 9
# Reno Night Life

At the time Reno was just beginning to explode, population-wise. Before then it had been primarily a tourist town that was also a university town.

As if that wasn't problem enough for the local police, you had to factor in cowboys. Northern Nevada had a lot of working ranches in Reno's vicinity and when the real cowboys came to town, they were a presence.

The biggest cowboy bar in town at the time was a place called the Shy Clown, and it was country, pure country. It had a room capacity in the thousands and on weekends, when the cowboys were in town, it easily exceeded that. It was huge.

The first night a group of the young European female dancers bravely ventured in proved to be a night to remember. There were about a dozen of them and they had heard about a place where they could actually meet real cowboys, and they couldn't wait. They had only seen cowboys in the cinema. Their female antennae were on alert and they were so very ready.

They came dressed to the hilt. Sable and some of the English girls had their flashiest Euro-attire on. Darcy and some of the other girls were dressed the way Dale Evans looked at her best. It was quite a show.

They walked in as a group, and for a brief moment, it was as if someone pushed an enormous mute button. Complete silence ensued—an enormous change from the noise level moments before.

All of a sudden, this group of male animals realized there was a new scent in the room, a scent they hadn't smelled before.

The first reaction was good. Handsome, young men in cowboy hats and tight jeans came over and the cutest one in front said, "Howdy, little ladies, can we buy y'all something to drink?" Darcy looked at Sable and with a twinkle in her eyes said, "This looks like a lot of fun".

What happened next wasn't. The biggest and toughest of the local rednecks weren't necessarily the most handsome or polite. That was when a true Old West barroom brawl broke out. Dozens of Reno's young men and cowboys ended up in either the hospital or the local drunk tank.

Not a good first impression by the locals. For the ladies, it was a rush, but hardly what they came for. Their fantasies of meeting real live cowboys were sadly dashed, at least temporarily. For the time being, they decided to stay with what was familiar: disco.

Disco was popular at the time, and the newest disco in town, the Magic Factor, was the rage. It was where all of the professional dancers in town hung out after work. The crowd was impressive.

Bars in Nevada can stay open twenty-four hours a day because of casino laws. The end result: after-hours was when the real nightlife got started. Casino employees on the swing shift got off around midnight and usually had a pocketful of tip money burning a proverbial hole in their pocket.

Cocktail waitresses, bartenders, and dealers came to see and be part of the show. The dealers were card dealers in various casinos, not drug dealers.

But drug dealers were also a big part of the town's nightlife. At the time cocaine was the drug of choice, especially for the night people. Sure, there was grass and Quaaludes, etc., but coke was the drug of choice at three in the morning.

However, it was common knowledge that the owner, Rick, was a former cop and anyone caught doing or even worse, selling cocaine would result in being barred from that disco for life. In other words, two guys in a bathroom stall together better be gay.

Strangely, this generated another interesting by-product. The really big drug dealers in town loved to party at Rick's disco. They never had to be bothered by gram buyers looking for an eight ball.

Most of them dealt in quantity and appreciated

the separation of work and play. They also made the best customers any bar ever had. Hundred-dollar tips were their way of saying thanks, and the servers loved the way they expressed their appreciation.

If a few of them showed up at the same time, the bar was wide open. "Crazy Eddie" would routinely buy a round of drinks for the house and would often light his hundred-dollar tip on fire. It happened often enough that the servers got the fire out before it reached the serial numbers. On any given night, the luckiest of the servers could pay their rent for the month.

The rest of the drug dealers came in all shapes, sizes, and colors. The one man they all feared and respected most was Achilles. He didn't get his name because he was a Greek god. He wasn't. He was African American.

Achilles was a huge man with enormous fists. His hands were the size of cantaloupes. Every finger on both hands was large and adorned with even larger rings. Just shaking hands with Achilles was an experience, kind of like trying to palm a basketball.

He got his nickname when he was a young man. According to the legend, Achilles was jumped by three members of a rival gang and beaten half to death.

After he healed, he hunted them down, one at a time. When Achilles was through returning the beatings, ten-fold, he cut each and every one of their Achilles tendons with a bolt cutter. All three of them lived, but spent the rest of their lives partially crippled.

No one ever knowingly messed with him ever again. There was a quiet danger about Achilles that was just plain scary.

One evening he and Rick were outside having a cigarette, when a foul-mouthed drunk clumsily stumbled into them. Amazingly, the drunk turned on Achilles and started calling him all kinds of names.

Achilles grabbed the jerk when he wildly took a swing at him. In self-defense, Achilles spun the guy around, kicked him in the butt, and sent him sprawling onto the parking lot.

Unbelievably, the jerk continued to verbally

embarrass himself until Rick had enough and started after him.

About that time the drunk decided it was time to leave the area and took off at a kind of run, except he kept tripping and banging into cars. He looked like he was running in potholes.

Less than an hour later the police were at the door to the disco with a warrant for Achilles' arrest for assault. According to the jerk, Achilles had hit him in the face a number of times. He was even wearing a neck brace.

When Rick found out about the charges, he took the officer in charge to the side. Rick told him, "In order to avoid embarrassing everyone unnecessarily, simply shake hands with Achilles. Examine his rings, and then decide who the liar is." It just so happened that the officer was an old friend of Rick's and had every reason to trust him.

Thankfully, the officer agreed. When he saw Achilles hands and rings it was obvious he had never hit the guy. Rick also told the officer that he had been a witness to the entire event and that Achilles had acted totally in self-defense.

Later that night, the jerk found out how kindly the local police took to false reports. Rumor had it, after he had a "religious experience," he decided to withdraw his complaint.

Back to the disco. The room was laid out in elevated tiers. The walls were covered with rough-hewn redwood which leant an earthy aroma to the room.

The cocktail tables were all the finest redwood burl with slabs nearly a foot thick. The seating was mostly director chairs with earth-toned fabrics.

The exception was one area off the entrance aisle that was set up like a Viking's castle. The couches and chairs were huge pieces of driftwood covered with furry hides. It was the VIP section reserved for professional dancers only.

The dance floor was elevated in the center of the room. The floor resembled a backgammon board with Tivoli lighting inlaid along the triangles. The lights in the floor, walls, and ceiling were capable of "chasing" in sync with the music.

Late nights, after the casino cabaret shows closed,

especially on the weekends, dancers from the shows would give their music requests to the disc jockey. Then they took over the dance floor with amazing routines, full stage make-up, and all.

Next, another group of pros from a different dance show would do the same and within no time, the dancing was like nowhere else on this planet. Eye-popping routines that often included some of the wildest outfits were the norm. At 2:00 AM the dance floor and the room were full, and people were waiting outside to get in.

From a dancer's point of view it was Camelot. It wasn't unusual to walk out of the bar only to realize the sun had already come up.

One other group to factor into the typical Renoites was the "ranch girls." Arizona has its Navajos; Reno has its "Nevadahos." Hundreds of young professional prostitutes live in the city when they are off duty. Many of the ranches are less than thirty miles away.

While at work, they are required to live in the brothels for extended periods. When they are off, they usually shared apartments with some of the other girls, much like stewardesses in large cities.

When they went out socially, they made up false alter egos. If you met one in a bar, she would never tell who her true employer was; instead they often said they were students or nurses. More often than not they said they were tourists visiting Reno for the first time.

Rick's disco was a favorite hangout for a lot of them. On any given night, there were often a surprising number among the crowd. If you didn't know who they were, it was impossible to tell.

When they were off duty they usually used their true names. At the ranch, they became Bambi, Trixie, or Little Bo Peep.

They rarely, if ever, came in alone. More often than not they would travel in pairs so as to be safe but not obvious. Getting one of them to go home with you was unlikely.

These ladies were professionals, and unless there is something very impressive about you, like money, diamonds, or limousines, the next level of relations was doubtful. Sex was work to them, but at the same time, most of them were looking for someone to take them away from "the life."

Like any other profession, theirs came with stories, stories about their customers as well as the everyday goings on.

For instance, the biggest ranch had just hired a new bartender. As was always the practice, every girl interested put a hundred-dollar bill in the kitty each week. The first girl to seduce him got the kitty. The kitty often ended up in the thousands of dollars.

It made being a bartender for the ranch extremely difficult. Dozens of professional ladies would do everything and say anything that might turn him on. Unfortunately for him, if he succumbed, he was fired immediately. Succumb they did, with regularity.

The ranch girls were also extremely generous customers. They made a lot of money and most of it was cash. They paid cash for their cars and they paid cash for their clothes and costumes. One of their favorite expenses was wigs. They had so many wigs; it was difficult to recognize them a lot of the time. “Big hair” was the rage and they were capable of huge hair in any color.

It really was the golden years of disco, and that room was a special place to be for those who were living their lives out at ringside.

Another memory was the night Darcy, Amber, and Sable went to a friend’s surprise party at Bad Bertha’s. To their surprise Bad Bertha’s was a “dykes on bikes” bar. The energy was high, the music was great, and despite the fact that they weren’t gay, the three of them had a great time.

Darcy even commented, “I don’t ever remember having this much fun without a man in the room”.

It was a night filled with fun until *he* arrived. *He* was the birthday girl’s former boyfriend. She left him because when he drank he got mean and violent.

He was obviously drunk, in a dark mood, and just looking for a fight. At least he was until he ran into Bertha.

There was a reason she was called Bad Bertha. She

was huge, the size of an NFL linebacker. She was a professional dominatrix who specialized in male masochists who liked to be hurt by a woman. It was a perfect fit.

When Bertha was through with him, as the song says, "He looked like a jigsaw puzzle with a couple of pieces gone."

Darcy, Amber and Sable stood back in awe as Bertha dragged what was left of him through the crowd while everyone kicked him and spit on him until at last she threw him into the gutter out front.

Something was wrong with his life. Not to say he got better, he didn't, but at that moment he promised himself he would.

Then there was the night the three of them went dancing with their friend Mike. Mike was flamboyant. He owned a women's boutique and he was more outrageous than the clothes he sold. The dancers loved him.

He was tall, good-looking, and had curly hair down to his shoulders. That particular night he was wearing a see-through vest and harem pants.

The four of them were at a huge disco called the Grand Ballroom. There was an enormous crowd and they were thoroughly enjoying themselves.

Sable and Darcy were in an unusually flirtatious mood and were having a great time teasing Mike, who was eating it up. Darcy turned to Mike and said, "I've never been out with a guy who was prettier than me before."

Unfortunately, a few of the local rednecks enviously decided Mike was not their cup of tea. They rode him unmercifully, calling him every name in the book.

Finally, Mike had enough and, pointing at the biggest of them, he said, "Okay, asshole, you and me, outside." The redneck didn't know Mike also taught martial arts.

The fight lasted less than three minutes. Mike walked back in to join the ladies. As he did you could hear the big redneck tell his friends, "Watch out for the faggot, he can fight."

A few weeks later it was New Year's Eve. It was the first New Year's Eve Darcy and Sable spent together. Both of the girls had that night off and they began partying early that afternoon at Rick's disco. By sundown they were high enough to hunt ducks with a rake.

Mike joined them and he suggested they move the party to downtown Reno to catch the rest of the action, he even offered to drive. Rick had to stay put to get ready for his first New Year's at his disco. So off they went the three of them.

Mike's ride that night was an old Chevy pick-up with bench seats. As they walked to his truck, he announced he was too drunk to drive. Sable volunteered.

The three of them climbed in with Sable behind the wheel and Mike immediately to her right. Darcy rode shotgun. That worked fine until they approached downtown.

At an intersection they were stopped at a red light. Sable saw a Reno Police cruiser right behind her and went into an immediate anxiety attack. To calm her down, even though he was too drunk to drive, Mike suggested they switch places; she could climb over him while he slid under her.

That worked fine, until Sable kneed the automatic

gear shift into reverse. As the light changed to green, Mike stepped on the gas and backed onto the hood of the police car up to its windshield. In retrospect, Mike said you have never lived until you've spent New Year's Eve in Reno's world famous drunk tank.

# Scene 10
# Soul Mate

Amber and Rick were in a one-on-one relationship from the first moment they met. Amber ran into Rick while out partying after rehearsals one night. They clicked immediately.

It just so happened that Rick owned the best disco in town. That didn't hurt. He wasn't a pretty boy, more of a Steve McQueen type, but they had this eye-contact thing from the first moment they met.

Rick had this smile; it just made her want more. At first she thought he might be too much of a ladies' man, but she found out he was perfect for her.

He was a fighter, a fucker, and a wild bull rider.

Rick was the typical bad boy women wanted to change. As she got to know him, she came to know he was the one for her.

The first night Rick and Amber spent together kept them up all night. It, for sure, was not a one-night stand. It was one of those nights that was completely unplanned but ended up being a life-changing experience.

A few nights later Amber had her first Friday night off and she was looking forward to being out for a night at his disco. She spent hours choosing just what to wear and getting ready. She was looking good and she was so looking forward to seeing Rick again.

Amber was in such a good mood, while she was fluffing and buffing, she sang and danced to most of her favorite Broadway tunes.

That was when it hit her. Amber got the worst leg cramp she ever had in her life. It dropped her to the floor. She literally had to crawl to the phone.

When she got there, she didn't know who to call. All of her roommates and closest friends were at rehearsal or out on the town. That left Rick. He was involved in Friday night, the busiest night of all in his disco.

Amber had only spent one night with Rick, an amazing night, a night like she had never known before. She was afraid to call him, she might blow it.

But this was urgent, she hurt so much and the leg cramps just got worse. She hated to, but she had to ask him for his help. Amber hardly hung up the phone and he was there for her.

Rick picked her up in his arms, carried her to his car, and again from his car to the emergency room, still in those wonderful arms. Amber was unable to walk, and somehow, having Rick's arms around her made it all feel so much better.

Once they got into the emergency room, they seem to have been placed on ignore by the "care givers." They were sharing a waiting room with a family who had a daughter who was bleeding, in pain, and crying uncontrollably.

More than too much time went by. Rick finally got fed up and approached the desk where doctors, interns, and nurses were standing around chatting and drinking coffee.

Their lack of concern lit him up. Rick told all of those within earshot, "You should all be ashamed of yourselves. People are in pain and you obviously don't care."

At about the same time, a big, fat security guard showed up. He opened with the classic question, "Is there a problem here?"

Rick's response was, "Yes, there is, and if you think you're going to solve it, you better call for back-up, because you won't even slow me down."

At about the same moment, the father of the bleeding girl showed up behind Rick and again let everyone know he was on the same side, he was just as pissed off, and as luck would have it, he was one very large, tattooed, scary-looking ally.

All of a sudden, everyone started moving. It was almost comedic, except for the fact that people were in pain.

For Amber, the pain went away in a hurry. After a quick examination, the doctor gave her a shot and she faded fast. As the drug took over, Amber looked into Rick's big blue eyes and said, "I love you. Can I keep you?"

It got the message across. Like a branding iron, he was hers. Rick knew she was under the influence but at that moment she was the most fragile, tender, beautiful creature he had ever laid eyes on and she was asking him to love her.

In truth, Rick really fell in love with her at a much earlier time. It was before he met her. Amber was dancing in his disco with her dance partner. Rick remembered the song they danced to was "Chattanooga Choo Choo," the disco version. Watching the two of them dancing together was amazing.

The way Amber moved and the way she looked into her partner's eyes left Rick feeling a yearning he never felt before. He had never seen fire in a woman's eyes, not like that.

It was at that moment; Rick promised himself he would do whatever it took to see a woman look at him that way someday. Here she was, that very same dream come true, asking him to love her. It made him believe he had fate on his side.

Ironically, they first bonded together so well because neither one of them wanted to get married. She wanted to dance until she couldn't anymore. He enjoyed to the max being a successful bachelor. As the song goes, "They had one thing in common; they were good in bed." As a matter of fact, they were good just about anywhere.

Rick and Amber built a relationship that was so amazing it wasn't at all unusual for strangers to walk up and compliment them on the love they showed for each other. It was a relationship that grew through the years.

It started with a passion for each other that was insatiable. They both had amazing appetites. That became love. Then they became the best of friends.

Rick and Amber ended up with the best of all three worlds. They wanted, they needed, and they enjoyed each other like too few people ever did. They had what everyone else was looking for and they were lucky enough to know it.

# ⚘ Scene 11 ⚘
# Special Ed

Ed was vice-president of the new hotel/casino and was in charge of convention sales. His friendship with Rick was a natural and they had become extremely close.

When Ed wanted to spoil his high rollers outside of his casino, he simply sent them in a limo to Rick's disco and everything was on the house.

When Rick wanted to play at Ed's casino, everything except gambling was on the house.

As an additional perk, Ed provided the casino limousines to transport the female dancers from the casino to Rick's disco after their last show.

Suddenly, dozens of gorgeous, tall, often European

women would arrive shortly after one in the morning. Rick absolutely loved it.

Talk about good for business. The first round of drinks was always on the house. The next rounds were paid for by guys waiting in line.

Ed usually came along in one of the limos. He was in his thirties and could party all night long. He and Amber became best buddies. It was always the three of them, Amber, Rick and Ed at the end of the bar, hanging out. The exception was when Darcy and Sable would show up. They both adopted Ed as a project.

Sable & Darcy took Ed on as a personal challenge; they were going teach him to disco. Night after night they danced and danced with him for hours on end.

That was until another woman caught Ed's eye. This was good for Ed; he loved being seen with beautiful women. It piqued other women's curiosity.

It was about that time Ed ran into Jessica. She was the ultimate vixen. He met Jessica at Rick's disco during a special black and white costume ball.

Everyone was supposed to be dressed in black and white. In her costume, Jessica violated every rule and showed up in red, white, and blue. That was Jessica, no rules, not ever. However, she made a better-looking Wonder Woman than Wonder Woman ever did.

Ed was perfect in his costume. He looked like either a choir boy or possibly a priest. It started as and became the perfect relationship.

As it turned out, Jessica was bisexual and preferred sex with her lady friend Terri and a male they both found attractive.

The two ladies were on the hunt that night. When they chose, Ed was the winner. Jessica's partner, Terri, was dressed as John Travolta, white suit, black shirt and all, that's where following the rules ended.

Ed didn't know he was the prey that night. He had no idea what he was in for. First Jessica hit on him in front of Terri, and then Terri came on to him strong. That was when Jessica said, "You don't have to make a choice, you can have us both."

All Rick saw was Ed smiling as he was leaving. Rick knew Jessica and Terri and what they were up to. It bought a smile to his face.

When they left the bar they proceeded to Ed's place. They didn't come out for two days. When Monday showed up it was too soon. Ed, Jessica and Terri all had places to go and things to do, none of which seemed so important anymore, at least not right now.

They had dinner together that night and decided it was time to make serious plans. There was absolutely no reason all three of them shouldn't be living together. Where was easy.

Ed had this huge house with lots of extra bedrooms so they all could have their separate, private spaces, while at the same time, they had common areas where they could enjoy each other.

It wasn't your typical relationship, but it worked for them. Most nights ended up with the three of them asleep in Ed's room, or as they called it, "the honeymoon suite."

Ed had found bliss. However, if his employers at

the hotel got any wind of what he was involved in, his job would be toast. They were extremely concerned with their image and Ed was flirting with disaster.

Rather than have that, he covered his trail perfectly. He alternated between his "better halves" while attending dinners and promotions. He was the envy of every man he knew.

As far as they knew, Jessica and Terri were rivals for Ed's attention. Nothing could be further from the truth. This was a relationship some people fantasize about. It certainly was not boring.

Ed's job also meant he had to entertain high rollers in a world-class manner. If they wanted to play golf in Vegas, the company jet was always available, pick the course. If they wanted dinner at the best place in Lake Tahoe, no problem, the limousine was waiting. It was one of those tough jobs someone had to do.

As a side bonus, everywhere Ed went, his money was no good, everything was comped. He was enjoying one of those times in his life where even though the days were incredible, the nights were even better.

Ed knew the nights they spent together would end soon, so he did everything he could to make every night special. That is why his lady friends started calling him "Special Ed."

When the company jet was free, Ed, Jessica, and Terri flew to Vegas to see the latest show. Anywhere his casino jet could go was their playground. It was a time in adult fantasyland. Ed knew a time would come when it all would change, but right now was what they lived for.

It came to an end too soon. Jessica and Terri decided it was time to have babies. In a separate discussion without Ed, they both admitted to each other they really did want to satisfy that weirdest of instincts, motherhood. They agreed Ed was about as good as they could hope for as a father.

When they approached him about their idea, Ed totally rejected the whole thought. He didn't want children, or at least not under the present situation, which was fluid, to say the least. To complicate it with children and the commitments that go with them was more than he was willing to make.

With that, a perfect relationship met its end. Jessica and Terri didn't require his presence any longer. They also did not need him to get either one or both of them in the family way. That would be no problem. Neither one of them needed a sperm bank to complete their mission. They moved out and moved on.

Ed was back on the bricks. Luckily, he had his old buddy Rick who not only owned the best bar in town but Rick was also was dating one of the most popular dancers in the new show, which happened to be appearing at his very own casino.

Wasn't there something Rick could do to help out poor old, lonesome Ed?

Amber came up with the perfect solution. In explanation, she told Ed, "The show has two performances every night with a two-hour break between shows. Since so many of the young girl dancers are from other countries and alone, why not have dinner with a different dancer whenever you feel like it?"

Give-it-away Ed had the power of the pen and

the house paid for exquisite dining in any of the seven gourmet restaurants. Rick and Amber accompanied Ed and his dates. Everything was included for free, except the tips, which Rick gladly covered. Dancers stood in line.

To a dancer, free food is a blessing. Free food from an upscale restaurant did make Ed a little more attractive, something he needed.

Ed wasn't really the handsome type, more the cherub type. He did know how to spoil a lady. Once a week and then more often, he indulged himself. After all there were hundreds of gorgeous females in the cast. He had a huge responsibility.

## Scene 12

# The Best Dance Contest Ever

When it came to disco dancing, Amber was the genius behind the scene. Before her professional dancing career began, Amber also had outstanding success competing in disco dance contests in and around Los Angeles. Not only did she compete, she won a lot more than her share.

Shortly after Amber and Rick started dating, she came up with an idea, "Why not put up the biggest purse for a disco dance competition that had ever been offered on the West Coast." Amber added, "Make it so huge, we can advertise from Los Angeles to Seattle." The results were so amazing it blew everyone away.

Nobody expected what came next. Hundreds of dancers came from everywhere on the West Coast. There were so many entrants; the qualifying rounds took weeks instead of nights. Combine that with the local competitors and their supporters, and the result was much larger than anticipated.

Amber was so excited she told Rick, "I want to be in the contest, too."

Rick responded, "That's not possible, we're sleeping together."

She thought for a minute and then asked, "What if we broke up for now?"

With a smile on his face he replied, "Just what do you think your chances of winning would be then?"

She decided to help with the judging.

Qualifying rounds were run during the week, so as not to interfere with the already busy weekend nights. Normally slower midweek nights now became hectically busy.

Crowds showed up at the disco to cheer on their favorites as well as to see the rest of the amazingly talented competitors. The room was filled to capacity night after night for weeks on end.

On the final night of qualifications, an enormous surprise happened.

Rick's last live-in lover, Tina, entered the contest by surprise. When Amber found out she was livid. Tina hadn't been around Rick since he ended their relationship. Now she was back and she seemed to have a scheme.

Amber was completely torn. She couldn't compete, but Tina could. The dance contest was her idea, and now she couldn't even be a judge. How could she? She couldn't vote for or against Tina and it made her furious. To top it off, Rick didn't seem to be aware of Tina's true intent, to get him back.

Amber not only disqualified herself as a judge, she left the disco for the night and went to her old apartment where she stayed up for hours listening to Gloria Gaynor sing "I will survive."

What she didn't know was Rick knew Tina and

just what she was up to. He also knew Tina was a fantastic dancer, capable of winning it all.

He knew there was no way he could legally exclude Tina, even if it meant a confrontation with Amber. Rick and Amber both slept alone that night.

All that grief about nothing. Tina's partner accidentally dropped her during a lift and she failed to qualify after all.

Even so, at her first chance, Tina made an attempt at getting Rick back. Rick was in his private office behind the back bar. Tina, as she had so many times before, walked right past the bartenders and into the office.

She closed the office door behind her. When Rick turned in his chair, Tina sat on the corner of his desk and began to strip from the top down.

When Rick asked her, "What on earth do you think you are doing"?

Tina cooed back, "I want another chance, I'll make it worth your time, I promise". Then she stood up and started to remove what clothes she had left on.

Before she could go any further, Rick grabbed her by the shoulders and with a hint of anger in his voice said, "Tina, you are one crazy fool. Our time together is in the past, not the future. You had your chance and you blew it".

When he told her she was crazy, it broke her heart and she decided to leave Reno for the last time.

Rick called Amber the next morning and asked her to meet for lunch. On the way there she feared he was going to leave her for Tina and the tears kept flowing.

By the time she got there, her eyes were puffy and red. She applied a little make-up, put on her big floppy hat and went in.

There he was smiling at her with those big blue eyes of his. Totally afraid of what he was going to say, she seated herself quietly, without their usual kiss.

He looked into her eyes and said "It's time we move in together. I don't ever want to sleep without you again. Last night made me realize how much you mean to me, and I can't stand being without you."

Amber practically exploded. She jumped out of her chair and onto Rick's lap and proceeded to kiss every inch of his face, much to the delight of the other diners nearby. Instead of moving on, Amber was moving in and she couldn't wait.

By the time the semifinals came around, the crowds had become so large; people had to be turned away. A room that was only supposed to hold a few hundred was pressed beyond its limits. It was the happening place to be, in Reno.

The night of the dance contest finals, the room filled up hours before the competition was scheduled to begin. There were eight couples left with a chance at the money. The anxious energy in the room was incredible.

To start the dance finals, Rick asked Izzy to help emcee the show. Izzy walked out to the center of the dance floor wearing a full-body silver jumpsuit. He had on more sequins than Liberace. Flamboyance was a way of life for him and this was what he did best.

When the audience quieted, Izzy thanked everyone for coming. Then he let out in his loudest voice, "Let's get ready to rumble" and the dancing started.

One couple after another offered their best performances, and they drove the crowd wild. It was live entertainment at its best. You could see it, smell it, hear it, and feel it in the air.

The audience came prepared. It was a night when the women of Reno put on the dog. Izzy wasn't the only one in sequins that night, and the coat check was full of fur coats.

When it was over, the audience stood and cheered, and then they cheered some more. It was an awesome display of dancing.

There was one moment that anyone there will never forget. It was at the end of Snowy and Julius's performance when they finished with the classic "death drop."

The death drop was a specific dance move where the male dropped the female in a 360-degree roll to the floor. Then he stopped her fall just before she hit the dance floor.

The two of them added a twist that tore the audience up. Snowy, the female, dropped Julius, the male, and stopped him at just the right moment. As Julius looked up, he smiled and winked at the crowd. They had the audience and they knew it.

Snowy and Julius finished first that night, which gave them the confidence and the money to enter the TV competition, *Star Search,* later that year, which they also won.

The couple that finished second in Rick's dance contest, Kathy and James, won *Star Search* the following year. Snowy returned to *Star Search* the third year with a new partner and again finished first.

The purse for those wins was a hundred thousand dollars each time. Back then, a hundred thousand dollars was a lot of money to anyone, let alone a dancer.

## ❧ Scene 13 ☙
# Male Strippers

Shortly after the dance contest finals were over, Amber, Darcy and Sable were watching one of those *PM Magazine* shows that did a short segment about a new club in Los Angeles called Chippendales and what made it unique: male strippers.

It occurred to them that if it worked in Los Angeles it should do even better in Reno because the local population was largely female.

Amber told Rick, "Men have *Monday Night Football*, shouldn't women have something special?" She added, "Only a man would put fantasy and football in the same thought," and there was no point in arguing. It was all her idea to try it out at his disco. Monday nights would be *Ladies Night*. As usual, her idea turned into a money maker.

The next step was to locate males who were willing to strip. That proved much easier than one would have thought. For the first show, ten professional male dancers Amber knew jumped at the opportunity. They made up their own characters and costumes and the show became the buzz of the nightlife.

Amber, Darcy and Sable were all there that night. They couldn't wait. They hoped everybody they expected would show up.

The first show was a complete sell-out. With absolutely no advertising of any kind, the women of Reno showed up in droves and they were dressed to kill, hundreds of them. It was a social happening. After a couple glasses of wine they turned from ladies into longshoremen.

Rick gave Amber a stack of one dollar bills and told her, "This is matches to start the fire. I expect the three of you to light up the crowd."

When the first dancer started, you could cut the sexual tension in the room with a knife. The air in the room was eerie, steamy, like a high school gymnasium.

It was obvious from the beginning that women were completely different than men when it came to strippers. Men at strip clubs act as individuals, one-on-one.

Not so with the female of the species. They hunt in packs. First Sable, then Darcy, then Amber, then a few more, and all of a sudden they all were standing in groups with dollar bills in their teeth.

The physicality or sensuality that happens is an over-the-top sensation. A young hunk is out there, and the ladies are ready to devour him like raw meat.

It made the front page of the *Reno Gazette Journal* the following morning, including a picture of one of the dancers. The picture was taken from behind the stripper, showing the faces of the women leaning forward trying to stick cash in his G-string.

As Rick was enjoying a Bloody Mary and admiring the article, the phone rang. Being the only one there, Rick answered. What he didn't expect came next in the form of pure rage. The caller demanded to talk to the owner.

When Rick responded that he was the owner, the caller started screaming on the other end. He told Rick that he was a lawyer and that he was going to sue Rick for everything he had.

When Rick finally was able to ask why, the caller, in a louder voice, asked Rick if he had seen the newspaper yet that day.

When Rick responded that he was looking at it right now, the caller said, "The girl in the center of the picture is my daughter, my sixteen-year-old daughter."

Taken aback, Rick told the caller that he had two off-duty police officers checking IDs at the door the previous evening. He asked the caller, "If you would, please check your daughter's purse before this gets out of control."

Somewhat surprised, the caller agreed. Ten minutes later the phone rang again. This time it was an entirely different person, or at least it seemed so to the ear.

In a much milder voice, the original caller said, "I am so very sorry. I checked her purse and she had her older sister's driver's license hidden away." He went on, "They look so much alike when she's made-up, that no one could tell the difference."

The caller continued, "She and I will have a meaningful conversation this evening. She has embarrassed this family."

Ashamedly, he admitted that his mother had called him earlier to see if he had seen the newspaper. She jokingly asked if he was aware that the women in every other generation in their family had been a little outrageous, including herself when she was sixteen.

Outrageous was what the male strippers were. One of them, "Little John" supposedly made John Holmes look like Tattoo. In real life, John was an iron worker who lifted weights all day for a living.

When John stripped, he did it for the attention and the fun. The money wasn't bad either. Then again there was the sex, which was his favorite part. He was an absolute tramp. He actually scheduled his women with stories like, "Is later okay with you?" His poetry would so overwhelm them that the usual response was, "Sure, when?"

The strippers, or "dancers" as they preferred to be called, stripped out of every costume imaginable. They borrowed costumes from their shows or rented them, or made them up themselves.

On any given night, you might see Darth Vader strip to his G-string. He could be followed by Superman, who would ceremoniously switch from Clark Kent to the Superman costume he wore under a business suit. Then he would continue to shred the shirt off his chest.

Next up was the cowboy, chaps, spurs, whip, and all. He was followed by the police officer, adorned with knee-high leather boots, handcuffs (fur lined), helmet, and mirrored sunglasses.

One of the dancers performed as a navy officer in full dress whites. He had the inseams of his pant legs lined with Velcro. When he reached the point where all he had left on was his pants, he did a dancer's bend from his waist, reached to his pants bottom, and proceeded to rip them off, bottom to top, leaving him standing there in all his glory, covered only in a white, satin G-string. The result was spectacular. One woman actually fainted.

Still another big hit was the construction worker. He stripped out of the full get-up, hard hat, tool belt, tight jeans, and of course the undershirt, which he ripped to shreds. When his jeans hit the floor there was an audible gasp throughout the room. He was a professional dancer and he had the legs to prove it.

"He has legs like a race horse," came out of one woman's mouth, and indeed he did. There were more than a few *Oh my Gods*, and as many more *Ooohs* and *Aahhs* and screams as well. He wasn't a handsome man, not at all, but at that moment he was lusted after by more women than Robert Redford would have been.

Still another of the most entertaining of the performances came as a surprise by the young man who was in charge of security for the bar. His real name was Bill, but to his friends, he was simply Dornbo. It was his takeoff on his favorite American, Rambo.

Bill was extremely handsome, just over six feet tall, and he had the body of an athlete. As a matter of fact, he was captain of the boxing team at the university. He was also editor of the school newspaper and had recently been voted "Best Looking Male on Campus."

The one and only time Bill performed, he stole the show. No one had ever seen him dance before, but the boy could dance. Bill was in a complete Rambo outfit, headband and all. He started slow, built to a crescendo, and left them wanting more.

Afterwards Bill said, "That was the weirdest feeling. All that passion was directed at me and me alone." He added, "I was afraid I was going to be raped hundreds of times." Bill did have that kind of ego.

These weren't necessarily the stars of the show as it evolved, but they were a great stop along the way. The real stars of the show were the audience. They were all sizes, shapes, and ages.

One young woman brought her mother and her grandmother. Nana, by the way, was the wildest of the group. Afterward she commented, "Forty years ago I would never have allowed my daughter to do anything like this."

Now they enjoyed themselves in a new, sort of sisterly way. Nana said. "My throat is sorer than it was after I gave birth to my daughter. I screamed then, too."

Another of the dancers was Jamey. He was barrel-chested and hairy. The guy drove them wild. Jamey wasn't much of a dancer. As much as he tried, including dance classes, nothing much worked.

Funny how women can be so forgiving of a stripper, for something they might feel negative about otherwise. Fred Astaire wouldn't have been nearly as successful as Jamey was.

There was a constant infighting between the better of the strippers. Nobody wanted to go first and everyone wanted to go last, with good reason. The tip money was much better later in the show after the audience loosened up.

When it came down to it, Jamey was the closer. There was just something about him that made them scream, and scream they did. He absolutely tore the audience up.

By the way, men were not allowed in the room until the show ended. They waited patiently, in line, outside the front entrance. They had to wait while all this screaming and shouting came billowing out through the front door.

The wait was well worth it. The women who remained after the Ladies' Night show were often in one of those "come hither" moods. That was when the party really got started.

The show was such a huge success, offers came in from everywhere. The best of which came from the owner of the largest bar in Monterey, California, a very upscale, wealthy, conservative city.

It was just one of those offers that included a private plane to pick up the crew, rooms at the best hotel, lots of money, and the plane back home. How could you say no?

Since no was out of the question, the dancers jumped at the chance and caught the plane.

The first night the *Magic Dancers* appeared, the place was sold out. Hundreds of Monterey's cougars showed up. It was an absolute riot, a huge success. Afterward the owner couldn't wait to up the offer. More money, rooms, and comps, what did it take? It was the biggest night of the year and he wanted more.

Two weeks later, the dancers showed up again. The show wasn't due to start until 8:00 PM. Three hours earlier Amber's alarm button went off. It was only 5:00 but she suddenly told Rick, "I don't know why, but I do know we need to go to the club now. Please trust me, I feel like something is wrong."

So off to the club it was. As Amber and Rick approached in a cab, they were surprised to see police cars all over the street near the entrance to the club. After they paid the cab, Rick and Amber learned there had been a riot.

Hundreds of women had been turned away at the door by the fire marshals. Over a thousand of Monterey's adult females had shown up to see the show. They stood in the drizzling rain for hours and waited. The marshals counted them as they entered the club. When the number of attendees exceeded seven hundred, the room's capacity, they cut off the line and told everyone else to go home.

Hundreds of Monterey's females who got turned away had enough. They didn't get violent, but they did express their civil disobedience.

Rick asked a young police officer what was going on and the officer responded, "I've never seen anything like it before. I'm not sure what caused it, but I just saw my mother and some of her friends leaving with the others, and I don't ever recall seeing her in such a huff. It was ugly".

With some effort, Amber and Rick got through the disgruntled crowd and into the club. Even though it was hours before the show was supposed to begin, agents from the Alcohol and Beverage Control board were there and grabbed Rick and the owner of the club and took them into the owner's private office.

It was there that the lead agent announced, "This show will not go on tonight."

Surprised, Rick asked him, "Why?"

The agent responded, "Monterey doesn't need this kind of smut and I will do everything in my power to prevent it."

Rick's answer was simple, "Show me a law that says these women can't enjoy the same thing men do right down the street."

As the saying goes, "The show must go on," and it did.

At exactly 8:00, Rick, attired in a three-piece tuxedo, walked into a room full of females who had been anxiously awaiting the show and asked a simple question, "Is anybody horny?"

The crowd went absolutely bonkers.

Once they settled down, Rick confided with the audience. "There are a bunch of men who do not want this show to go on. They are here in the room. You can see them. They are the ones in the suits and ties. We need your help to keep them away from us so we can give you what you came for."

There was an audible gasp in the room, followed by what can only be described as a group growl.

The suits could feel the heat, or was it the heat that felt the heat. At any rate the suits backed up, way up. They ended up so far away from the dance floor you could hardly see them.

Then the show started. Little John went first and he was never better. Dancer after dancer performed the best they ever had. Jamey closed and the room went absolutely crazy. The noise level was so loud it hurt your ears.

As Rick was smiling at Amber, so proud, an agent from Alcohol Beverage Control advised him he was under arrest and escorted him to the same private office again.

Once there, the lead agent advised both Rick and Blake, the owner of the club, of their Constitutional rights, per Miranda.

When Rick asked, "What are we being charged with?"

The lead agent responded, "Blake has his own set of problems; his liquor license is history. For you however, we have criminal problems as well."

Rick, with a silly smile on his face asked, "Really?"

The lead agent proudly responded, "You incited a riot and caused an obstruction of justice."

Rick responded, "When did I do that and please tell me what did I do?"

The lead agent replied, "When you identified my men and made them withdraw for fear of their lives, that's when."

Rick smiled and said, "Can I quote you on the part about being in fear of their lives?"

At that point the lead agent ordered his men to handcuff Rick and not the owner.

Rick stood up, extending his arms in front of him, and said, "Please do, you are about to make me a wealthier man."

Confused, the lead agent hesitated, and then asked, "What are you talking about?"

Rick cockily retorted, "Tomorrow's headlines all over the West Coast are going to read, *Male Strippers Arrested in Monterey.*"

Rick added with a twinkle in his eye, "All I can

say is, thank you so very much, we are going to be seeing a lot of each other".

The good news was the lead agent backed down when he finally realized Rick meant what he said. The bad news was the club's owner got scared and that was the final show for the *Magic Dancers* in Monterey.

Long story short, the male strippers were a huge success, so much so that an entrepreneur with a lot of venture capital made an offer to buy Rick's disco and the rights to the *Magic Dancers*. The offer was way over the top and the bar sold. And it sold for a lot of money. Even the negotiations that led up to the sale were fun.

## Scene 14
# After Magic

The buyer made his first offer one night at the bar, which is a total no-no. Drunks always wanted to buy the place until they sobered up. This guy was different. He suggested they meet the following day over dinner, at his expense, and when he suggested Harrah's Steak House, the three of them agreed when to meet.

Prior to the meeting, Amber and Rick talked it over and figured the bar was worth about $250,000. At dinner, the buyer started out by offering $350,000. Rick countered, saying he thought it was worth closer to $450,000. Amber shot Rick a look that could fry eggs; then she kicked him under the table and it hurt.

He felt better quick when the buyer agreed to

Rick's terms, provided Rick would carry the balance for one year at a reasonable rate of interest. Afterward, Amber, with her big puppy dog look, said, "I'm sorry about the kick."

With a big grin on his face, Rick said, "Not me, I hope it leaves a scar. That way we will never forget this night."

With that money they were able to begin a new life together. Since Amber's dancing contract had expired she was footloose and fancy free. Immediately after the disco changed hands, Rick and Amber married in a small wedding chapel in Reno and caught a plane to Mexico for their honeymoon.

Even though their luggage was lost for a few days, they hardly noticed. It was the best honeymoon ever. That is, with one exception. The third night they were in Mexico, Amber and Rick attended a special sunset champagne party put on by their hotel.

After a few glasses of champagne, Amber was feeling a little loopy when she said to Rick, "I absolutely love it here in Puerto Vallarta. Do you want to know why? It's the ideal place because we're a thousand miles away from all of your ex-girlfriends and I have you all to myself."

She no sooner got the words out of her mouth than Tina showed up out of nowhere and let out a loud, "Rick." Amber almost died.

Then Tina introduced them both to her new husband and everything seemed so much better. Amber did proceed to have a few more drinks and a very good night.

Early in their marriage, Amber told Rick, "We are much more likely to die poor and generous instead of rich and greedy."

Amber wasn't usually wrong, but this was the exception. Generous they were all of their lives, but poor they were not.

Amber and Rick started early buying real estate; first a duplex, then a triplex, and eventually ended up owning a half-dozen very large apartment complexes, a summer home at Lake Tahoe, and a winter home in Maui.

Home is an understatement. The "lake house"

was a modest mansion on the shore in North Lake Tahoe.

It had its own boat pier. At the end of the pier there was a boathouse complete with an electric crane. When the boat wasn't in the water, it was in its own little house completely out of the elements.

It wasn't just any boat either. It was a Chris Craft that was used by smugglers in the days of prohibition to move liquor from Nevada into California. In its day it could outrun any boat on the lake.

The main house sat on acres of land that were beautifully landscaped. Almost every month of the year different flowers were in bloom except when it snowed. Because the property slanted downhill from the street to the lake, at street level the house was two-story. By the time it reached the lake, it stood three stories tall.

The most impressive room was at lake level. It was three stories high with custom-made windows that ran from floor to ceiling. The huge glass panels formed an enormous bay window overlooking one of the most beautiful views of Lake Tahoe.

The great room featured one of the three enormous rock fireplaces spread throughout the house. The ceiling was supported by dark, natural wooden beams.

The house in Maui was enormous with a pool and a year-round staff of live-ins. The ocean views from every room were spectacular.

Sailing around the islands on their boat called *Dancer* was the best. Life was good; really, really good.

Amber and Rick loved having breakfast at Longhi's Café, where they drank the best Bloody Marys and dined on the freshest of crab omelets.

For dinner, it was the Swan Court; where stunning black swans paddle within reach of the diners. When Amber commented to the waitress that it was the most beautiful place in the world, the waitress responded, "Dats all we got" with her beautiful Hawaiian accent.

They stayed for a month or two and then flew home to Lake Tahoe for a month or two, only to return again and again.

Rick and Amber vacationed whenever and wherever they wanted. Cruise ships were a favorite.

They weren't just in love, they were, but they were also the very best of friends. They really got each other. Rick had this way of looking at Amber that made her heart race.

Amber and Rick trusted each other, respected, and honestly believed in each other, as well as each other's abilities. Abilities were their long suits. Performing arts, dance, and professional choreography were but a few, and that's just Amber. Rick had a zest for life and enjoyed every moment.

Rick loved life and Amber, and Amber loved Rick.

Between them there was little they couldn't or didn't do. Theirs was a true soul-mating that lasted a lifetime and longer.

One night, after seeing an off-Broadway show in New York, the most unimaginable thing happened. Amber and Rick were approached by a drugged-out, deranged young man who demanded their money. Amber had her purse strapped over her shoulder so securely that when he grabbed and yanked, it threw her to the ground.

Rick, in his late fifties at the time but always the bad-ass, attacked the intruder with everything he had. What he didn't have was a knife, and suddenly he realized blood was coming out of him, a lot of blood.

The killer took off running in a hallucinogenic panic.

It was the most horrible moment in her life as Amber watched Rick slump to the ground. She crawled to him and held his head in her arms. He looked at her for that last time with so much love in his eyes, and then he was gone.

Amber looked up at the sky and cried, "Oh God, please don't take him." Her life changed forever in that single moment.

Amber had to face tomorrow without Rick at her side. For most of her adult life she had been half of his whole. Now all that was left were the memories of a lifetime of love fulfilled beyond her wildest dreams.

That was then, and this was now. Amber was boiling over with talent and determination in spite of her loss. She had a wonderful past and she knew the future was full of promise as long as she tried.

She knew Rick would want it that way. Amber had so much more to give; all she needed was the right chance.

Amber always would feel that Rick was out there, watching over her.

That was when she opened the mail one day and there was this invitation to attend a twenty-five-year reunion of the first show she appeared in. It would reunite Amber with her dearest old friends, Darcy and Sable. The invitation seemed to be telling her now was the time to move on.

# Scene 15
# The Divine Darcy

In Darcy's case, her personal fate had been predetermined without her knowledge before she even moved to Reno.

Over a year before meeting Amber and Sable, Darcy had appeared on the TV game show *The Price is Right*. She not only appeared, she won. She won everything, including two cars, one of which she gave to her boyfriend, who, by the way, was a complete jerk. His name was Charles, not Chuck, and he sold yachts in San Diego to the rich and famous.

When he had a hot client, he would have Darcy pose on the prospective yacht in a bikini. Sadly, he told her to "Phut the shuck up" when buyers were around. He was not the sensitive type, much like her father. It seemed like a real good time to get rid of him and she did. "Here's a car, see ya later."

What happened as a result changed the rest of Darcy's life. The IRS showed up in Reno about eight months after the big show opened.

When the IRS agent asked her why she hadn't declared her winnings from *The Price is Right* as income, she responded, "You're joking right? Please tell me you're joking."

The agent glared at her and in a very icy voice said, "The IRS does not joke."

After all, she only won about $30,000. That was when they explained about penalties and interest.

When she realized how much she owed, Darcy had two choices the way she saw it. First, she could bow down and beg her father for it, which was totally unacceptable, or second, she could accept an offer to dance in Paris for Madame Bleu and spend the rest of her life as an ex-patriot.

As soon as her contract in Reno was up, Paris it

was. Darcy became a true Parisian for most of the rest of her life. One door closed and another opened.

Just to begin with, Darcy danced as a lead in the largest shows in Paris for the next few years. At the same time, for the fun of it, she tried out modeling. That became a gold mine, too.

For years Darcy was employed as the face of one of the largest cosmetics firms in Europe. Her face, in a variety of poses, was on cosmetic boxes everywhere you turned.

Because of her extremely long legs, she also became a runway model for the biggest designers in Paris. In addition, as a cover girl Darcy adorned the cover of most of the elite European magazines again and again.

One success led to another and during her prime Darcy was one of the most sought-after icons in Europe.

With fame came success, and with success came wealth. Although Darcy never much cared, inevitably she amassed a small fortune of her own.

Just for the fun of it, Darcy joined an all-girls rock and roll band and, as usual, stole the show. She couldn't play guitar, but she pretended to. Darcy also wasn't much of a singer, so she lip-synched most of the time. At times they turned her microphone off.

None of that mattered because Darcy was so knock-down, drag-out gorgeous no one in the audience seemed to care. The rest of the ladies in the band actually were very good, enough so that they traveled with some of the biggest headliners in Europe as an opening act.

It was while Darcy was a rocker she met her future husband, Mykal. Although he was German by birth, Mykal had lived all of his adult life in Paris.

When they first met, it was anything but love at first sight. In their very first conversation, Mykal told Darcy, "Americans are truly selfish and ugly," and he blamed them for just about everything.

In response, with a flash of anger in her eyes Darcy stated, "European men are arrogant, self-centered, and extremely overrated as lovers."

Mykal was intrigued by her but had no idea who Darcy was. He was completely unaware of the fashion industry and rarely, if ever, paid any attention to style magazines.

To him, Darcy was a tall, good looking redhead he found unusually attractive. He had always had his way with any woman he wanted, but this one was different. This one grabbed his attention and wouldn't let go.

Mykal struck Darcy in much the same way. He was handsome, very much so, but there was something more. When Mykal looked into her eyes, Darcy felt like he was touching her insides. It was an eerie feeling, like nothing she ever experienced before. Darcy remembered thinking, "I've got goose bumps. This is interesting."

Hate became love and they began a life filled with all of the good things two people in love, in Paris, can have. Six months later Darcy and Mykal were married before a local magistrate.

Mykal owned a small restaurant in the City of Lights. It was nice and quaint, but barely making a profit. Darcy had some Southern California ideas and with her financial backing, she helped to completely make over the restaurant.

The restaurant was three stories tall on a hillside overlooking the river. For some reason, Mykal used only the middle floor. The restaurant was successful, but not nearly as much as Darcy could imagine. She saw so much more promise.

Darcy talked him into turning the bottom floor into a piano bar, which was, more or less, unknown in Paris at that time. She added in some of her dancer and modeling friends and dressed them in sexy red satin dresses, slit to the hip. They became hostesses, cocktail servers, and singers, and people began lining up out front.

Once the bar and restaurant were packed to the brim, Darcy simply moved on to the third floor, which she transformed into an elaborate disco. In no time at all, it was jammed until all hours of the night.

In a very short time, the modest little restaurant that was barely making it became the hottest night spot in Paris. Profits doubled and then doubled again.

Mykal and Darcy ended up owning, at one time, five of the best restaurants in Paris. Combined, their restaurants routinely served thousands of meals every day.

Darcy's primary role in the operation of the restaurants was to "work the room." She was the epitome of a social butterfly. Darcy had become fluent in three languages besides English and would bounce from table to table throughout the rush hours; the clientele loved her.

It was considered the highest compliment when Darcy would join them, even if only for a few moments. This also brought up the camera concession. A picture of Darcy sitting with you and yours blessed the walls and desks of countless Europeans.

Eventually, Mykal and Darcy took managing partners into each of their restaurants so they could enjoy their lives without all the work.

Enjoying life was something they did well. Mykal loved soccer and bicycling and Darcy loved sports and painting.

They traveled throughout Europe for years,

watching their favorite teams compete. They stayed at the nicest hotels and ate in the best restaurants.

When they ate, they drank, and when they drank, what they drank was most important. They usually preceded dinner with one of their favorite champagnes. Red wine with dinner, French red wines of course, only the best. Price was never a consideration for them except for one time.

While in the south of France they had heard of a restaurant by the name of Le Petit Pier, which sat on a small pier over a beautiful lake. Mykal and Darcy were both impressed with the décor.

Every effort had been extended to make it appear to be out of the times when kings named Louis ruled the land. It was extremely well-done to the smallest detail.

When the wine steward asked for their order, Mykal said, "Don't bother with the wine list, just bring the best bottle of champagne you have."

The steward leaned over and politely advised Mykal that the best champagne they had to offer was bottled before Napoleon was born and its cost would be in the thousands of dollars, American.

Somewhat embarrassed, Mykal smiled and asked to see the wine list after all. That was the only time that happened. From that moment on, he always asked for the wine list.

Darcy carried her oils and her easel with her everywhere. Her paintings were so good one day Mykal suggested, "Why don't we display some of your artwork on the walls of our restaurants?"

It took her by surprise. Darcy didn't realize how good she actually was. Despite all of her acomplishments, underneath it all she was truly a modest person.

Darcy was so well-known because of her modeling career, collectors and investors began buying them up faster than she could finish them, at very unconscionable prices. It turned into another gold mine.

Whenever they could, Darcy and Mykal preferred to travel around Europe in their own railroad car they converted into a rolling luxury condo. It was an antique car from the late nineteenth century.

They completely stripped the interior and made it into the latest almost futuristic home. It was complete with kitchen, satellite TV, and every other indulgence they could cram into the limited square footage.

They lived their lives with a style that was all their own. Darcy and Mykal often joked that they were like children without parents to tell them no.

Unfortunately, it was their lifestyle that ended Mykal's life during his fatal fifties. When they were at home in Paris, Mykal loved to have his close friends over for Saturday brunch.

They lavishly gorged themselves on every rich, calorie-filled pastry Mykal had made fresh that day. Next, they all climbed on their bicycles and rode off.

Darcy watched her man and his friends ride off on that beautiful, sunny Saturday and she thought to herself, "*I'm the luckiest woman in the world,*"

On a normal day, Mykal and his frinds would ride for hours. Not on that day. It ended abruptly when Mykal suddenly keeled over. It was a massive heart attack. He was dead before he hit the ground.

At that same, exact moment, Darcy felt like something grabbed her. For no apparent reason, she sat down on the floor and began crying. Less than an hour later, Darcy got the news of Mykal's demise and she realized she'd been in the grasp of the angel of grief. Darcy was completcly devastated.

In the weeks to come, she went through every emotion there was. She was hurt and confused. She was extremely angry while at the same time so very lost. The two of them had been so co-dependent on each other, his loss left her without half of her reality.

Darcy hadn't even balanced a check book in over twenty years. Thankfully, the restaurants they owned were on automatic pilot and required nothing from her.

Darcy really had no idea how much money they had, let alone how many investments. That wasn't her concern, not ever. Darcy had always been more than happy when Mykal bought her a new car every year. That was all she needed to know.

With the help of their family lawyers and accountants, Darcy was amazed to find out that they were millionaires many times over. In addition, there were the five restaurants, which she decided to sell to each of the managing partners.

Those partners, who could, paid cash. To those who couldn't, she loaned them money, on her terms, which were more than fair.

All five of the transactions worked out to the benefit of all parties concerned and Darcy added millions more to her bottom line.

Darcy tried to ease the pain of her loss by traveling like the two of them had to places they had been together. She revisited Rome, Venice, Berlin, and a dozen other cities. But Darcy was so lonely, it didn't work. It just made it worse, so she returned to her home in Paris.

In the depths of depression, Darcy opened her mail one day and among the letters of condolences, she found this incredible invitation to attend a reunion in Reno.

Reading that invitation brought Darcy back to life. It was like a light came on after being out too long. The despair left her and a smile came out for the first time in a long time

Darcy suddenly had this strange feeling come over her, like Mykal was standing there telling her she should go and never look back.

It was time to get on with her life and she finally knew it.

Darcy couldn't wait to see the two people in the world she really missed, especially now, Amber and Sable, what a terrific surprise.

## Scene 16

# The Sensational Sable

Speaking of Sable, God gave her one of the most beautiful bodies he had ever given anyone. Unfortunately, with it came a terrible curse, her total inability to reach that magic thing called orgasm. It haunted her throughout her life.

She tried, they tried, everyone who ever got that close to her tried everything. She and her lovers spent an enormous amount of time as well as a fortune on sex toys. Nothing worked. She liked it all, but nothing, absolutely nothing, worked, not that way.

Combine that difficulty with the kind of uncommon beauty that makes men in pursuit of a trophy wife go crazy, and the result was a recipe for disaster.

Her first husband, Vito, was a world-class downhill skier. He ruled the Alps for a decade. No one could beat him.

Vito's classic Roman face and body had gained him international respect. In his beloved Italy, he was a god. His rumored abilities as a lover were Casanova-like. Women threw themselves at him so often, he became jaded. That was until he first met Sable.

One look at Sable and her aloof beauty, and Vito came on to her like a panther. She was impressed and he was completely smitten.

Vito was so taken with her that for the first time in his life he asked a woman to be his wife. When Sable said yes, he thought all of his dreams had come true. He was certain they would grow old together.

Unfortunately, trying to get her off grew old much sooner. Vito had never met anyone like her. Try and try again, nothing worked.

Part of the problem was that Vito made Sable

promise that she would never pretend, and "never" can and did become a terribly destructive word.

Try as they might, it just didn't happen. Sable really wanted it to, but to no avail. The more she tried, the more she failed. As much as Sable loved Vito, and as many times as she tried, it just wasn't going to happen. It destroyed her as much, or more, than it did him.

In the end, Sable realized that it was Vito's reputation as a lover that had attracted her in her endless attempt to find satisfaction. Unable as they were to succeed, the marriage was over almost as soon as it began. That was when Sable found out about his affairs with other women.

The rumors and tabloids finally got to Sable and she confronted Vito face to face. At first he denied the reports, but guiltily, he finally admitted he had cheated on her, a number of times. It made her feel like she was a failure.

Sable's divorce settlement was huge, ransom to keep Vito's reputation as a lover intact.

Money didn't matter to him; he had more than he could ever spend. Vito's reputation as a Casanova was the one thing that was all-important. This way, neither one of them had to accept their failures, at least not publicly.

Husband number two was a real sheik. Not just any sheik, but a man with dark, exotic good looks to boot.

Ali had become modernized and had foregone wearing the traditional Arab attire. He was more at ease in a suit made by his favorite English tailor.

Ali owned a yacht that was so large it looked like a small cruise ship. It had two helicopters, three decks outside, and more below. It had three swimming pools, including one indoor.

It also had a spa, complete with sauna, gymnasium, and massage rooms. The ship's crew included two masseuses that were available twenty-four hours a day.

Off the formal dining room there was a large music room as well as a piano bar and lounge. The cinema sat up to fifty and there were five incredible luxury suites located on decks two and three. Each suite had its own private outside balcony.

The entire enclosed area of the top deck was the master suite, which was topped by a retractable glass roof. Touch a switch, and the entire ceiling would disappear. Even when it was closed, it was the clearest glass, and seemed to be full of stars.

Ali kept the yacht in the south of France, usually docked in Monaco's yacht harbor.

Sable and Ali actually met in Monaco during the Grand Prix. Sable loved racing and Ali loved gambling. It happened after an exciting day of watching the race.

Sable was relaxing over cocktails with a girlfriend when her friend Mary pointed Ali out sitting at a nearby table.

Mary couldn't wait to tell Sable all of the local rumors about him. She said Ali was enormously wealthy, a graduate of Harvard Law School, and a notorious cad with women.

Allegedly, Ali had taken three working girls to

his bedroom at once and had worn them all out before he was through.

Mary's obvious interest in Ali gained his attention and he came over to their table and asked permission to join them.

Mary, salivating at the chance and playing less than hard to get, practically begged him to sit down. Unfortunately for Mary, it was Sable he was after, and after in a big way.

Ali ordered a bottle of his favorite champagne, and after a few glasses, he informed them he was having a bit of a soiree on his yacht the following night. He asked Sable and Mary if they would like to come as his guests. Mary immediately said yes, but Sable declined. Sable was more than interested, but didn't want to be as obvious as her friend.

Ali agreed, but expressed his disappointment, and then promised to send his limousine for her friend the following day at 6:00 PM. He also told Sable if she had a change of plans she was more than welcome to join.

After listening to her friend plead with her for

hours on end the following day, Sable finally agreed and off they went in the limo to the heli-pad. From there it was a short helicopter ride to the ship, short but still a rush.

Sable wasn't at all surprised when they arrived at his yacht and he told them the rest of the guests had cancelled at the last minute. Ali was extremely apologetic that there would be just the three of them.

Mary bubbled out, "That's great, more to go around."

Sable thought to herself, "*More to go around is just what I'm afraid of.*"

Long story short, Ali completely ignored Mary, and she got drunk and passed out on a couch.

Sable, on the other hand, had never been wooed in quite such an exotic manner. She didn't want to let on how affected she really was. So she sat quietly with an elusive smile on her face and it drove Ali wild.

When he couldn't stand it anymore, Ali asked her straight out what it would take to get her to go to bed with him. Ali wasn't abrupt, quite the contrary. He was polished, educated, and smooth, and women never told him no.

Ali was astonished when Sable said, "You would have to marry me first."

He told her she was crazy and she agreed, she probably was, but nevertheless that was what it would take.

Despite Ali's family's bitter protests, they were married ten days later in a little chapel near the casinos, the same casinos where he spent most of his waking hours.

Unfortunately, as addicted to gambling as he was, Ali spent most of his time away from Sable. When Ali gambled he didn't even use casino chips, he used large multicolored discs instead. Don't even ask what each disk was worth. Ali's income from his family's oil fields was so enormous, he couldn't spend it as fast as it came in, try as he might.

Ali did have those nights dreams are made of. When he won, he won more money than most people could imagine. When he lost, he lost more than most people could cope with in their worst nightmares.

The first year of Sable and Ali's marriage was bipolar. They had laughter and love, but they also had battles that would send the servants scurrying for cover.

On the day of their first anniversary, he and his entourage had left for the casinos early and Sable had the ship all to herself.

She started with a Swedish massage that took over an hour. That was followed by a facial, a sauna, a soak in the Jacuzzi, and a long, hot shower. Next, her hairdresser took her time getting her hair just right.

Now it was time to apply her makeup. Sable's eyes and the way they were made-up were very personal to Sable. She had been presenting them in her special way since she was a child. At this point in her life, she knew exactly the colors she wanted to use.

Eyelashes were her favorite. Sable had lots of her own natural eyelashes and she owned lots more. Tonight didn't call for Bambi eyes, but for something a little less. Blackest of black mascara, dark smoky eyeliner, and rich charcoal shadow brought out her ice-blue eyes like never before.

A touch of shimmering highlight just under her brow created the perfect exotic look Sable was going for.

Then it was time to choose just the right gown for the evening. Finally, the jewels and Sable was ready. One last look in her dressing mirror brought a smile to her face and a glow inside.

Tonight was the night Sable was going to tell her man he was going to be a father. She'd known for a few weeks, and she was bursting with anticipation. She couldn't wait.

Sable heard the helicopter land and she glided up to meet him. Her plans were crushed when she saw Ali. He was in a fury.

Ali had lost way too much money and made a scene at his favorite casino. The scene he made was so outrageous the casino manager asked him to leave and even suggested that he stay away for some time.

Ali was darkly silent at first, and then he snapped. He broke statues and destroyed paintings worth a fortune.

Ali began screaming and yelling in his native tongue, then he turned on her with his fists clenched.

Ali came at Sable slowly, and he so terrified her she started to panic.

Sable pleaded with him to stop, which only served to upset him more. Then Ali resorted to violence. Ali slapped her so hard she fell against the wall. He hit her again and again until he was exhausted.

Ali beat Sable only that once, but that was more than enough.

The more he hurt her, the more she withdrew into herself. Sable hated Ali for that more than anything else.

Even though Sable screamed for help, again and again, none came. The crew knew better than to interfere in his personal affairs. Ali paid them for their silence and he paid them very well.

The beating ended and Ali immediately left and fled in his helicopter out into the night.

In Sable's whole life, no one had ever hit her like that. Sable was emotionally spent and physically numb.

Lying on the floor she began to weep out loud. Finally, one of the female crew members was brave enough to come to her rescue. Sable was unable to stand on her own, but together they managed to get her to a couch nearby.

When Sable looked back at the floor where she had been, she froze. There was a pool of blood where she had lain. She gasped. She was losing her baby. Then Sable passed out.

When Sable came to, she was in the local hospital in a VIP suite. Sable awoke to find a doctor and two nurses hovering over her. The first words out of her mouth were, "The baby, please tell me my baby is okay."

From their expressions, Sable knew the worst had happened. The baby was gone.

Because there was no one she knew there and

there weren't any flowers, Sable asked where her husband was.

The doctor informed her that the hospital had been unable to reach Ali since the "accident." They weren't even sure if he knew what happened.

They told her their yacht was still moored in the harbor, but no one had been able to reach Ali.

Sable asked when she would be able to leave, and when the doctor said, "We would like to keep you here for a few days," she laid into him with language he hadn't heard from a woman before.

With a look that frightened him, Sable icily stated, "No, I am leaving right now," and leave she did.

Sable made a brief stop at the yacht to collect everything of value she could carry. She filled her suitcases with diamonds, rubies, pearls, and all the cash in the safe. She skipped the clothes; she was in a hurry.

Before Sable left, she told the captain of the ship he should let Ali know that she miscarried his baby.

Sable despised the captain and his crew for not coming to her aid. She felt it would be poetic justice that he would be the one to deal with her soon-to-be ex-husband. Her thoughts were, "Oh, to be a fly on that wall!"

Husband number two didn't contest the divorce either and was ultimately most generous with an enormous cash settlement in exchange for her silence.

Ali didn't appear in court, and she never saw him face-to-face again.

After two marriages, Sable agreed with Zsa Zsa Gabor's famous quote, "I never hated a man enough to give his diamonds back."

Then along came Cary. Cary was an international playboy. He looked like and was named after Cary Grant.

Cary was incredibly good looking and, to top it off, he was a real charmer. The combination was overwhelming to most women.

Cary always seemed to have a suntan and he loved ballroom dancing, so much so he had polished a reputation as one of the best ballroom dance judges in the world.

That was how and what brought Sable and Cary together.

After her second divorce, Sable decided to pursue her fantasy to be a photographer, and she approached it as an art form. She took classes all over the world from the greatest professional photographers at the time.

More often than not Sable got her tutoring for free in exchange for some modeling efforts. She read, studied, and applied her art.

Within ten years, Sable was offered her first private showing at a prestigious photo gallery in New York City.

While Sable was preparing for the display, she needed a break and decided to attend one of her favorite pastimes, competition ballroom dancing.

The national championships were being held in Madison Square Garden, near her hotel. So Sable did what dancers love to do, she got dressed to the nines.

Sable had so much fun choosing just the right outfit, she began to feel renewed. After another hour or two of prepping and primping, she was ready; boy was she.

She had been in a funk for too long. Sable almost forgot what it was like to know you really look good, but tonight she looked great and she felt special.

When she got to the Garden, her spirits reached an all-time high. Sable walked into that enormous room filled with thousands of the "beautiful people" and she absolutely glowed. Sable felt her best and it showed. Everywhere she walked, heads turned.

When Sable passed the judges table, Cary saw her for the first time, and for the first time in his life he was breathless, unable to speak.

When she passed by, Sable turned and smiled at him, and he saw those beautiful ice-blue eyes and Cary practically melted.

Not to say it was one-sided; much the opposite. Sable had never seen such a warm smile and something about him made her a little weak in the knees as well. It was electric.

Cary watched Sable get to her seat and at the first break he couldn't wait to approach her. Cary was so taken by her uncommon beauty that he had difficulty focusing on the competition.

Sable saw Cary coming towards her and couldn't stop grinning. From that night on, they were together.

Cary courted Sable in a most impressive way.

On their first date Cary took her for a ride in a Hansom horse-drawn carriage around and through Central Park. They drank champagne and he told her some of his favorite stories. Sable felt like Cinderella with her prince.

The first night they slept together Sable approached Cary with her little problem up front. His response was, "What's the problem? As long as we're together, everything else will be great."

Sable cherished that moment. True love had finally found her.

Cary's family was all about the oil business, had been for generations. They were deeply entrenched in every aspect of the whole business.

Besides drilling and exploration, they also had become the largest supplier of related equipment in their part of the world. When the Alaskan Pipeline was built, his family was one of its main suppliers.

Cary's family was enormously wealthy, enough so that they had their own fleet of airplanes.

Every member of the family, and there were many members, had their own private jet. Each jet required two pilots on call 24/7. The family actually employed more pilots than a few small commercial airlines, and they paid their pilots even better.

Their home office was in the suburbs of Los Angeles and they kept their planes at a small private airport on the outskirts.

The family reunion at Thanksgiving was quite

impressive the first time Cary took Sable home to meet the clan. Everyone was there that weekend. As they were all arriving, it looked a bit like O'Hare Airport at Christmas.

The family members poured out of their jets and into another fleet, this time chauffeur-driven stretch limousines, escorted by the local police, to the family compound.

The compound itself sat on a "modest" sixteen-hundred-acre estate. The main building was over three hundred years old and was a classic example of what you could do with an old Spanish casa grande combined with an unlimited budget and incredible taste.

It was as large as it was stunning. Although some of the buildings were newer, they had all been kept with the original design, white-washed stucco walls with red tile roofs.

Overall, there were nearly twenty buildings on the compound, including the very latest in stables, garages, and extremely luxurious servants' quarters. Calling them "servants" was not accurate. They were treated as well as family. The houses they lived in were opulent, to say the least.

But, even so, none stood out more than the main house. It had dozens and dozens of rooms and a grand staircase that was nearly fifty feet wide. Despite the Spanish exterior, the interior was marble and granite and plush.

It was ruled over by Cary's grandmother, Olivia. She was a true grand dame. Olivia was petite, but so much larger than other people on the inside. Generations of wealth and power had ended up in a gene pool that produced her.

Brains and beauty were Olivia's weapons of choice. If you can picture the most beautiful, elegant woman you have ever seen, and give that woman the brightest mind you have ever encountered, that was Olivia.

Men did not rule this domain, Olivia did. She was nearly seventy years old, but she still had the beauty that could turn men's, as well as women's, heads.

Olivia, like her mother and her mother's mother, dominated their men, all of them, husbands, brothers, sons, it didn't matter. There was never any question who was in charge in this family.

Olivia had been born to financial royalty and raised to become its leader. This, like so many other dynasties, was totally matriarchal.

She knew it was now time for her to find her replacement, but, try as she might, she couldn't find any likely candidates among her heiresses. The males were weaker than the females (what's new?). These females had not been hardened, not like she needed them to be.

It was at that very moment when Sable walked into the room. Sable entered with a presence that was so impressive, she reminded Olivia of Audrey Hepburn as Eliza Doolittle entering the ballroom in *My Fair Lady*.

It was love at first sight. Sable and Olivia locked eyes across this vast room filled with an ocean of people, and it was as if everyone else disappeared. It was just the two of them.

Olivia felt a warmth come across her she hadn't felt in years. It was her. Sable was that one. It was like the love of a woman who always wanted a daughter and never had one, only to receive one late in life.

It also didn't hurt that Olivia previously had Sable checked out by her security people, when she suspected Cary was getting serious. Olivia already knew everything about Sable.

There were two major things about Sable that most impressed her.

First, Sable had put together a financial portfolio that was bigger and better than Cary's. That was important because she knew Sable wasn't after Cary for his money. Even though Cary was more than a millionaire, his total fortune was slight in comparison to Sable's.

Second, Sable had been a professional dancer, a fantasy of Olivia's since she was a child, a fantasy unrealized because of her position. Being a dancer had always been her number one fantasy.

At that split second in time everything changed. It wasn't just the moment, but the bond. Olivia saw the beauty in Sable's eyes, and she knew the true value of what Sable had to offer.

Olivia knew Sable was someone above and beyond the rest. As it would turn out, she was right. Sable was exactly the right person to show up at just the right time.

When Sable finally appeared before her face to face, they were both visibly affected. Absolutely nothing had affected them like this before; not Olivia, not Sable.

Olivia looked into Sable's eyes and she knew what had absolutely enchanted Cary. She knew now that her favorite rogue was about to be wed.

And so it went, Cary and Sable were married that spring. It was the number one event of the season. Being on that wedding invitation list, let alone the reception, was almost impossible to achieve. It was bigger than a royal wedding.

The skies were full of helicopters. Paparazzi were everywhere but were kept at an extreme distance by a private security force that specialized in lavish celebrations. This was a domestic security team that was the best money could buy.

But then that would describe the entire wedding. Chefs were flown in from all over the world. Wines and champagnes came out of the family cellars and flowed like rivers. The elaborate wedding cake was six feet tall. Sable's dress was designed and handmade in Paris, and featured over a thousand hand-sewn pearls.

When Sable entered the church for the first time, it was as if a vacuum sucked away every noise in the room. When her bridal music came on, she glided down the aisle with an incredible amount of panache.

Sable had the presence and stride of a dancer, and even through her veil, they could see she wore a smile that told everyone in the room she was happy, so incredibly happy.

For Cary's part, he was devastatingly handsome in his black tuxedo with tails and a white ruffled shirt that contrasted his dark tan and lit up his gorgeous white, toothy smile.

When Cary lifted Sable's veil and saw her amazing face, he couldn't help himself. Tears of joy trickled down his face, but he never stopped smiling. It was the happiest moment in his life.

The next year and a half they were inseparable: Sable and Cary at night and Sable and Olivia during the day. Sable and Cary were the talk of the town in Los Angeles. They were A-listed everywhere. It was the best time of their lives.

Ironically, Sable and Cary first became attracted to each other because neither one of them ever wanted to get married, or in Sable's case, ever again.

They both had been extremely successful as singles. It wasn't until they got to know each other that it was so much better to be part of a whole instead of alone.

That was when it finally happened. Sable was so incredibly happy that they had faced her problem together, and she was more than enough for him. For the first time in her life she didn't feel like she had to try so hard and/or fake the results.

Sable and Cary loved being together and just cuddling one night when one thing lead to another and Sable finally relaxed while making love with her man.

She'd given up on orgasms when she never expected what happened next.

Sable suddenly felt this unusual shuddering

feeling and then it hit her like a freight train. She had an involuntary spasm and this astonishing feeling shook her entire body, not once but again and again.

When they finally wore themselves out, they started laughing, out loud, without abandon. From that moment on, her little problem was no more. The bond between Sable and Cary was set in granite for life.

From breakfast to afternoon tea, Sable sat at the feet of Olivia. She learned who she should trust and those she should not.

Olivia opened up her heart and her mind to Sable like she never had before with anyone else. Olivia taught her about the really good people and those that weren't. Two of those lessons would become so important too soon.

Cary, the love of her life, the yin to her yang, was gone in an instant. The car accident wasn't Cary's fault, but just the same, Sable was left with an enormous void; he was dead.

For once in her life she'd found love with the right guy. Cary understood her and she adored him.

One moment later and he was gone. Life seems to treat gifted people that way all too often.

Sable lost more than her soul mate. She lost the one man who really loved her. She felt more alone than ever. Her parents and family were, and always had been, dysfunctional. That was putting it mildly.

Cary was her best friend, her mate, her lover, and now he was gone. She was a complete and total emotional wreck.

In stepped Olivia and everything changed. At first they cried together. When that passed, together they decided to do something good in Cary's name, something that would last.

With that began the brainstorm that would eventually become the most famous performing arts school in North America.

## Scene 17
# Academy of Performing Arts

It was Olivia's idea. She decided it was time to put the family estate to better use. More often than not, Olivia was the only one who lived there. There were dozens of live-in domestics as well as gardeners and chauffeurs. It was not Olivia's only residence; she had others all over the world.

In a moment of sheer genius, with her connections, Olivia took a remarkably short time to achieve the accreditation they needed, and the Cary Diamond Academy of Performing Arts drew its first breath.

Olivia called in lifelong markers from her

politician friends. They owed her so much more, they were more than happy to help out.

The architects came next, followed soon after by an army of engineers and construction workers. They turned buildings and barns into the most gorgeous dorms ever seen. They weren't really dorms, more like high-end condominiums.

Getting involved with the design of the academy, helped get Sable's mind off of her loss. She began looking forward to the events of each day. Sable, personally, oversaw every step of the construction as she watched the academy come together.

Everything was the latest. The computers, which were everywhere, were state of the art. The rooms were furnished by the best decorators in Los Angeles and were just plain luxurious.

The main building was converted into classrooms that were big and roomy, while at the same time comfortable. It was redesigned to use every inch to its maximum capacity. The main staircase was surrounded by cameras and was the setting capable of everything up to and including a remake of *Gone with the Wind*.

An entirely new building was designed and built to include a performance stage that utilized all the latest gadgets in sound and lighting that were available anywhere in the world.

Studios were everywhere, with hardwood floors and mirrors from floor to ceiling and often on the ceiling as well. Music recording and filming were available in every studio on request.

There were dozens of soundstages located throughout. They weren't only soundstages but were also capable of producing anything from demo tapes to ready-to-play CDs and DVDs.

Everything in the entire complex had been converted to be completely powered by solar energy. It did happen to be Southern California, where the "sun shines every day."

There was not only no power bill, but also their design was so efficient, it produced enough power to sell back to the local power company at an excellent profit.

Directors flew in from Broadway. Acoustic technicians came from all over the world. Engineers were imported from NASA to help with the carbon footprint. When the geniuses were done, the end product was world class.

Money had been no object and it showed. There was no place like it anywhere in the world. In its final form, it would change not only the realm of entertainment education, but also the efficient use of energy itself.

The future for so many would begin here; it was hard to believe that it started in the hearts and minds of Sable and Olivia.

Next was the solicitation of students, the greatest students anywhere in the world.

Olivia and Sable decided to advertise for the first class anywhere their voices could be heard. They used the press as well as the Internet. They used television and radio. They bombarded the youth of the world with an outrageous offer.

The total cost of advertising to the academy was extreme, but their plan was to do it just that once. If Sable and Olivia were successful, the rest should, and did, fall into place. It was a multimillion-dollar investment, but it ended up a winner.

Thousands and thousands of students worldwide applied. The most outstanding applicants were invited to audition. Those few who were accepted received a complete education as well as training in their own artistic specialty for free.

Lodging, meals, tuition, and first-class health insurance were all paid for by the foundation endowment set up in Cary's name. Literally, every expense you could conceive of was paid for. Sable and Olivia's master plan was maximum reward for maximum effort.

As if that in itself were not enough, the staff of instructors was the envy of the industry. The pay structure was so generous and the work conditions so ideal, it attracted the elite of the true young geniuses of the time from all over the world.

No one else could compete. Olivia and Sable got anyone they wanted, and they wanted only the best.

Olivia lived to see her dream come true, but shortly after the academy opened, she died quietly in her sleep. She had been ill for some time prior, and her death came more as a blessing than a surprise.

Just at that time, as fate would have it, out of nowhere came an invitation to attend the reunion in Reno. Sable couldn't wait to see the best friends she had ever known. All of a sudden, Sable missed Amber and Darcy more than ever.

## Scene 18
# The New Beginning

Now here they were, Amber, Sable, and Darcy. All three had more than a few properties and investments of their own, but all three had been left alone, something that wasn't their making.

Each of them had lived their lives, being in love with their best friends. Now they were each alone.

It was at the reunion that Sable approached Darcy and Amber with an idea. She needed their help to add the final touches to perfect her performing arts school.

She really needed them. Sable had no idea of Amber and Darcy's wants and needs at the time, but she felt she must make them an offer. It just so happened, to her surprise, the timing was perfect.

Sable started the inquiry with, "What are you doing the rest of your lives?" She went on to tell the whole story of the academy. The more she talked, the more interested they both became. By the time she was through, Amber and Darcy were sitting on the edge of their seats.

Sable didn't show her age on the outside, but on the inside, time and heartbreak had taken their toll. She really missed and needed the camaraderie she had known with Amber and Darcy. Not to mention they were also incredibly talented and exactly what she needed to complete her dream of a performing arts school.

Sable told them she really hoped that it would rival Juilliard. The East Coast had Juilliard, the West Coast deserved as much or more. After all, where else would you go to learn dance? Los Angeles was where the road led for many dancers and musicians with a dream.

Amber was first to ask, "When can we start"?

Darcy chimed in with, "Count me in too. Let's do this. I can't wait".

The investments and properties Amber and Darcy owned were easily put under management companies and they were off to join Sable. It became a time of friendships renewed and accomplishments achieved.

Their mothers would have been proud of them. However, all three of them had already passed on.

Sable's mother Remy had died first. She was the one who had lived on the wild side. Besides Sable, Remy had five other children, none from the same father and none even resembled the others in any way.

Dinner at their house looked like a meeting at the United Nations. Sable spent most of her young life caring for her younger siblings and was more of a mother to them than her mother ever was.

Sable began dancing in one of the local strip clubs when she was so young she had to lie about her age. If they had known how young she really was, instead of what showed on her false ID, it would have changed her life.

She was physically developed beyond her years, and she needed money to help care for her family. Her mother often got drunk and went on a runner for days on end.

Sable felt so sleazy that first day at the strip club, but when the asshole in charge said "Show me your tits," she did, and she blew them away. Tits she had. Tits like they had never seen before.

Sable got the job, and with it came more money than her family had ever seen, a family that had seen very little.

Within a month Sable was a headliner. Her tips went up, as did the cost of going to the backroom with her for a private lap dance. She danced under the name Betty Boops, and she became a star overnight.

Sable was such a hit, the manger decided to run a picture of her in a newspaper ad campaign they were trying out. They even put up a giant glossy poster of her out in front of the building.

It was all so exciting until Sable's mother found out.

Remy went absolutely ballistic when she discovered what Sable was doing. What Sable was doing was what her mother said got her into the bad situation in the first place. The difference was Sable knew how to do "it" without having babies.

Sable became an expert at giving pleasure to men. Unfortunately that was a one-way street for her. Men couldn't give her that pleasure in return.

Later in life, under therapy, Sable realized that was the time that changed her sexuality. Because she had to do "it" to provide for her family, she lost all ability to connect to the rewards that should have come with it. Add to that her "loving" step-father and if frigidity had a cause, Sable had hers.

Bailey, Darcy's mother, died early as well. Her end result was her refusal to have mammograms. Breast cancer killed her, and it seemed so unfair. Like Darcy, she never was given much in the way of breasts, but she still got breast cancer.

Bailey, like the other two mothers, adored her daughter. But, because of Bailey's relationship with her husband, she wasn't able to teach Darcy what she really knew about men and being in love.

In their last conversation together before she died, Bailey told her, "Darcy, the man you think is your father, actually isn't. Your father never knew that the summer you were conceived I was on vacation with two girlfriends. That was when I met your real father. We immediately fell in passionate love and one thing led to another."

Bailey went on, "He had the most beautiful emerald-green eyes I ever saw. Every time I looked into your emerald-green eyes, I saw him and it made me love you all the more. It was a summer love and by the time I found out I was pregnant, he was long gone and I had no idea at all how to reach him."

Bailey reached over and grabbed Darcy's hand and with tears in her eyes admitted, "When I found out I was pregnant I had to decide between an abortion and marrying the man you've know as your father. He had always been persistent in wanting to marry me. So without ever telling him the truth, I agreed."

"We flew to Las Vegas and were married in a wedding chapel by someone who looked like Elvis. We enjoyed a short three-day honeymoon. It really wasn't so bad, but I have to admit that I fantasized that I was with Matt every time I was in bed with my husband".

Looking down Bailey admitted, "Darcy, of course, you were born "prematurely. No one ever questioned it."

At first, Darcy was taken back. Then she realized that her mother, the one person she loved so much, had carried this dark secret around with her all of her life. It broke Darcy's heart knowing that her mother felt so much shame.

When Bailey begged Darcy for her forgiveness, Darcy told her with all the love in her eyes, "It makes absolutely no difference. As a matter of fact, I like the idea of being a love child."

Darcy wanted to know everything about her natural father. She even admitted to her mom, "I always had a fantasy dad, a dad who treated me with respect and really loved me; things I never felt from Dad. Those were the things I so desperately craved."

Bailey told her that they met at a dance and how much he loved to dance. She said that at first sight he seemed very gangly. He was tall and thin and had these long, long legs, but boy, could he dance. He told her his love was ballroom dancing. His name was Matthew.

Bailey noticed him dancing with someone else before. Matt was so good that when he first asked her to dance, she felt intimidated. But it was summer, a beautiful night, and everything felt so right.

The next thing Bailey knew, she was spinning around this huge dance floor and all she could see was Matt. She'd never known what it was to dance like that. He was so good. Matt not only led perfectly, he followed just as well. When Bailey wanted to express herself, once she was comfortable enough, he let her.

They were so good together, she couldn't see anyone else. Then Bailey realized why. The dance floor had cleared and everyone was watching them. She had never had a moment like that in her life, and quite honestly, she loved it.

When the dance ended she was so embarrassed, in a wonderful way. Everyone was smiling and clapping. Apparently, the magic Baily and Matt had shared had been voyeuristically enjoyed by everyone else. It just didn't get better than that in her life, it never did, and at least for now Bailey was his.

After a while they got away from the crowd and took a walk down the beach. The moon was full, it was a warm, beautiful night, and Bailey had feelings she'd never experienced before. Just holding Matt's hand made her feel so special, she couldn't stop smiling.

That was when Matt kissed her. She'd been kissed before, but never like that. Bailey's heart raced so much she was afraid he would hear it. There was a lifeguard's boat upside down up the beach where they could be alone and that was where Darcy got her beginning.

Bailey's lovemaking experience was extremely limited, but it didn't matter that night. Matt took her places she had never been, good, tender, loving places.

Matt didn't just make love to her—he *enjoyed*

making love with her, in a way Bailey had only dreamed of. Not just once, but again, and then again, until they fell asleep in each other's arms.

When they woke, the sun was up and early risers were just beginning to hit the beach. Bailey and Matt quickly dressed as best they could and tried to make a discreet exit, marred only by the evening clothes they were wearing, as well as a couple of very sheepish grins.

That was how they spent the next few days. It could have lasted forever, but as things happen, it didn't come to pass that way. Matt suddenly had to return to his home for a family emergency, and for reasons Bailey never learned, he didn't return.

It was the tenderest moment that Darcy and her mother ever shared and it was, sadly, also one of their last. Bailey slipped away before they had any more time together.

Amber's mother, on the other hand, found love again in her later years. When Marian was a young mother, Amber was the center of her universe. For nearly twelve years, she drove Amber to dance classes, tap, jazz, and ballet, and just about any other dance class there was.

They couldn't afford private dance lessons when Amber was young, so Amber did the next best thing: she got dance class schedules for all the park and recreation districts within fifty miles.

After school and all weekend, as well as all summer long, every summer, Amber took every class she could. Her mother became her full-time chauffeur.

Marian wasn't just indulging Amber. She was vicariously living out her childhood dream, a dream to be a professional dancer. Marian became what she called "a chauffeur to the star."

Marian remembered her mother. She was the one who made it to Broadway, and she remembered the thrill of being backstage in the wings watching her mom dance.

Marian's mom was only in the chorus, but that didn't matter in any way. Marian experienced what the stage had to offer and she was hooked forever.

Unfortunately, before Marian got the chance to go on her own, she got pregnant. Marian was going to do whatever it took to make it possible for Amber to have the chance that she had missed out on.

Amber and Marian both adored Shirley Temple movies. It wasn't that rare that one would be on TV during the school day and Amber would hide until her dad left for work. Then Amber and her mom would cuddle up on the couch and watch. They not only watched, they danced.

Amber's mom even taught her how to tap dance like a pro. Marian truly loved everything about Amber and had big plans for her future. Marian was a bit of a stage mom.

When Amber was barely a teenager, she approached her mom and in a completely honest way asked, "Am I dying?'

Alarmed, Marian asked her, "What on earth are you talking about?"

In explanation, Amber poured out her darkest fear when she said, "I think I figured it out. You give me everything I ever dreamed of including love, I get more than any of my friends. So much so that the only explanation is that I must be dying and you're not telling me. Am I right?"

Marian was so blown away, she took a moment to compose herself so as not to laugh out loud and embarrass her precious daughter. She smoothed her apron on her lap then grabbed Amber in a bear hug.

She pulled Amber over until their faces were inches apart and said, "In all your life you have never been more wrong. You are such a goof. You are in perfect health, but I do have to admit, you do have one heck of an imagination."

Embarrassed and relieved, Amber gave a little chuckle and said, "Are you sure?"

Many years later, Amber's father died after a long battle with cancer. As soon as possible, Marian sold her house in Detroit and rejoined her darling daughter in Reno.

She began a metamorphosis and left her caterpillar shell behind in Detroit and never looked back.

When Marian arrived in Reno, she decided to

move into the finest, most expensive retirement community there was. Marian wanted to be close to Amber, but was determined to get a life of her own for the first time in her adult years.

Marian underwent liposuction and had some nip and tuck work done on her face and neck. She looked like and felt like a brand-new woman. It was there and then she met John. He was tall, dark, rich, and good looking. Every widow and every divorcee in the place were after him.

That competition ended when Marian moved in. With her new look, a complete new wardrobe, and rediscovered confidence, she seemed to sparkle, which didn't go unnoticed.

It happened slowly, but happen it did. John learned to love Marian in ways he never loved his first wife, and he loved only his first wife, all of her life. That was then and Marian was now.

John was a retired executive with the CIA and had incredible tales to tell. They were inseparable and she became his "belle of the ball." For her part, he was the love of her life and she knew how to appreciate him.

Seven years later, after moving to Reno, cancer took its toll and Marian passed away. To Amber it was an enormous loss, but also made her so happy because she got to see her mother blossom and truly enjoy the last years of her life.

## Scene 19
# The Finale

Moving back to Los Angeles was easy for Darcy and Amber. After all, that was where they began their friendship.

They were too set in their ways to consider being roommates at this point in their lives. They did, however, buy mansions within a mile of each other and close to the academy.

As Darcy and Amber took up their parts in running the academy, they began to realize what an enormous undertaking Sable had already accomplished. They also found out how much more there was to be done.

Teaching students was only a small part of what they needed to do. Running the business side of the school was such a huge task, they knew they needed help.

To get the perfect person, they used a local, high-profile headhunting, agency. The agency provided them with ten prospective resumes, which were arranged in the order of best qualified.

While they were looking through the candidates, Darcy was the first to discover Special Ed's vitae among them. She turned to Sable and asked, "Could this be the same guy"?

Sable took his file and broke out laughing, "Sure it's him. He's put on a few pounds but otherwise he looks great."

Amber took the file and couldn't help herself when she asked Sable, "Didn't you use to have a crush on him"?

Sable came back with, "You know me; I had a crush on just about everyone".

The three of them had not seen Ed since those wild and wonderful times they shared in Reno nearly thirty years before.

Sable, Amber and Darcy went through the motions of interviewing all of the candidates and held Ed for last. What he was requesting in the way of compensation was more than the rest; however, he did bring much more to the table than any of the others.

Through the years Ed had developed contacts with corporate sponsors and he was well-known as one of the most successful fund-raisers in the country.

When Ed arrived for the first interview, he had no idea what to expect. He couldn't even fathom what an exclusive academy would need him for. Ed didn't have a clue.

That was until he walked into their office, and there they were, three of the most favorite friends he had ever known. Ed had lost touch with them all when they went their separate ways, but there they were.

Ed was smiling so big, his smile muscles hurt. After all the hugging and kissing was over, they got down to business.

Sable told Ed, "The original endowment money

was intended to pay operating expenses as well as scholarship funds. The amount of money that had accumulated in addition is staggering. That is where we need your expertise."

Ed had no idea he was walking into one of the most challenging opportunities of his life. It was what he had trained for and worked for all of his life, and here it was on a platter. They easily arrived at an agreement and he was off to do his thing.

Although all three of the widows had been successful, Sable, Amber and Darcy were somewhat naïve when it came to investing that much money properly. Almost all of the funds were in low-yield, secure mutual funds.

Ed's stock market experience as well as contacts finally paid off. By splitting the funds in three different, higher yield accounts, he more than earned his pay. As a matter of fact, the changes Ed made increased the academy's nest egg three-fold in a very short time.

In addition, Ed arranged for corporate donations to sponsor the good work the school was doing. He created a financial empire that ensured the school would not only survive but also prosper forever.

Ed even obtained funding for the largest and most modern film library in the world, which became the newest addition to the Cary Diamond Academy.

When the film library was completed, it was the proudest achievement of Ed's life. What he didn't know was that the three widows had secretly decided to name the film library after him.

Ed didn't find out until the day of the dedication. Sable, Amber, and Darcy insisted on driving him to the ceremony. When they got there, they blindfolded Ed and walked him from their limo to the podium.

All of a sudden, the school band broke out in his favorite song, "Rocky's Theme" and Amber removed his blindfold.

As his eyes adjusted to the light Ed realized he was looking at his own name, at the top of the film library, carved in marble letters, six feet tall. When it finally sank in, Ed started to cry, something he never remembered doing before. But there he was, tears streaming down his cheeks.

It fulfilled a dream only he knew about. Ed had never married, nor had any children. His secret fantasy was to leave something behind to prove he had been on this earth.

At his age, Ed didn't know how, but here it was, where artistic geniuses would see it for all time. He felt overwhelming pride and fulfillment well up inside of him like he had never experienced in his life.

Speaking of pride, Sable, Darcy and Amber knew the feeling that day. When their good friend Special Ed, the tough guy, broke down in tears, there wasn't a dry eye anywhere.

Tears flowed, make-up ran, and noses, well, noses did what noses do when you cry. Between the laughter and the sniffling, the bond of love and appreciation between the four of them absolutely glowed.

Next, it was time for them to put on a show that displayed what they had achieved with their students. It was their opportunity to show the public what their academy had accomplished. The theme of the performance was "The Best Show Ever," and that's what it was.

Promoting the event was so successful, representatives from all the major talent agencies came, and ended up getting a lot more than they expected.

Everything was original, including the music, costumes, and choreography.

The first year-end production started with original music written and performed by the students. It included all styles of music; jazz, blues, classical, pop, rock and roll, and country. As the opening music ended, the curtain came down.

After a short break filled with applause, the curtain and the music came up again. Suddenly, the most amazing dancers flew across the floor in an array of styles that showed how dance evolved over the last one hundred years. It included dance styles from the flappers to modern day hip-hop and everything in between.

The choreography was unique in the way it blended the music to the abilities of these incredibly gifted dancers. Each number was better than the last and when they got to the finale, they reached an incredible peak, and it was over. Over, except for the standing ovation that followed.

There they were, Amber, Darcy and Sable, holding hands with tears streaming down their faces again. Even though none of them had ever had children, they knew it had to feel something like this. They were so proud. They felt like Judy Garland and Mickey Rooney in the old movies; they'd done it, they had put on the *best show ever.*

## About The Author

R. Douglas Johns still keeps a home in Reno, Nevada, "The Biggest Little City in the World". Between 1978 and 1980 he owned the hottest disco in Reno.

During that time Reno was a boom town. Several new hotel/casinos opened at midnight on the same day including the Sahara, the Money Tree, Circus Circus and the MGM Grand.

With the new casinos came the huge production shows that brought professional dancers and singers to Reno from all over the world. It was an exciting time filled with amazing shows, both large and small, as well as an incredible night life scene.

It was a golden era in Reno, new night clubs were opening and R. Douglas Johns was right in the middle of it.

The author took liberties creating this fictional story based on the lives of three beautiful young dancers. Names, characters, places and incidents either are the product of the author's imagination or are used fictitiously. Any resemblance to actual persons, living or dead, events, or locales is entirely coincidental.

For information, book orders, and to offer your input, visit our website at:
www.DancersReunion.com